T0365968

All
For
A
Dream

All
For
A
Dream

Sandra Lee Brand

Archway Publishing books may be ordered through booksellers or by contacting:

Archway Publishing
1663 Liberty Drive
Bloomington, IN 47403
www.archwaypublishing.com
844-669-3957

ISBN: 978-1-6657-6963-1 (sc)
ISBN: 978-1-6657-6964-8 (e)

Library of Congress Control Number: 2024925444

Print information available on the last page.

Archway Publishing rev. date: 12/12/2024

I dedicate this book to my husband in Heaven. I also dedicate it to the following: Gretchen Boehme who is my most treasured editor and friend whose patience and skill are beyond words and my special friend Colleen who allows me to read it to her long distance to edit and expand the content. I thank my neighbors for the children who surround me and make me laugh and think. They are the models Ariellah, Mark and Gabriella, in this book. They are also the constant reminders of why I treasure the minds and thoughts of these little ones.

CHAPTER 1

T HE MORNING STARTED OFF WITH EXCITING NEWS FOR THIS HAPPY little family of four. Maria, the mother, had explained with patient clarity, as mothers feel is necessary, "Isabella, our big girl, is going to be ten this year. Izzy, you will be in double digits! Your father and I have found a bigger apartment. We don't want you and your brother to continue taking turns sleeping on the couch or sharing the bedroom. So, my sweet girl, you can help with this expense. Don't worry, you won't have to get a job! Daddy and I have both gotten raises and if we don't have to pay anyone to get you up and ready for school, we can afford it. You will be closer to your school so that you can walk. This is how you can help. Do you want to do this big girl thing?"

The response was, "OH YES! Please. I am getting old enough to do more to earn my keep! I want to help!" Isabella, better known as Izzy, glowed with excitement. Mother and daughter laughed with joy at this declaration. Izzy was so very ready. Life was good and getting better! Young Isabella felt that she was quite rich. She loved her life. She could now walk Matteo to school instead of having her parents pay their morning sitter to do that. She was going into the double-digit zone of responsibility very soon. Who knew ten would make you so grown up and responsible? The best news of all was that she would not be ten for a few months, but she was starting the walk of responsibility early. There were so many exciting responsibilities owned by the oldest in a family.

She felt she could handle anything asked of her. She was almost ten and her parents trusted her. Could anything be better?

They were living the American dream and were officially on four wheels now! There were so many wonderful events for this little family. America was, indeed, a land of opportunity. There are responsibilities that need fulfillments for all to be citizens. These are not to be over-looked, but...

Matteo's addition to the family vocabulary was the word "Kiddos". He wasn't a child. He was a kiddo. The kiddos observed this new purchase of their car with rapt attention and barely suppressed excitement. Matteo said, "So, more money is a very good thing. How can I help make money, too." His little face looked puzzled when everyone laughed.

Daddy picked up his handsome boy and they spun as one around the new "used" car. "Ah!" remarked Izzy, "We are rich indeed!" Izzy's long dark red hair reflected the sun as she and her mother joined the joyous event with a spinning dance behind the male celebrants!

They had come to this country to work and become citizens. The children had been born here so they were Americans. Next on the list was to review what was left to be done to make the parents Americans, as well. They knew they were behind in this quest but had been working so hard and kept pushing this need back to be done when time permitted it. They were driven to "be all they could be." Demanding work meant success.

Now this new car was going to be initiated with the first ride being to school. Then the adults would head for work. How could life be better…. except, maybe a bit more chocolate in their diet? Maybe this would be a reason for another family chat, thought the youngest kiddo who was a huge fan of chocolate.

Because Matteo was so excited about his first ride and it was to be to school, he was eager for school. After this initial ride, the two children would walk together to school. Matteo was told that he was to hold his sister's hand and follow her directions until he turned ten and then there would be another talk about responsibility. Matteo asked, for clarification, "But, Mama, when I turn ten, I will still be younger than

Izzy. She will just keep on having birthdays to stay ahead of me. When will I be in charge?"

Maria looked at her lively inquisitive son and answered, "You will know when that time is here as you learn more and grow. One day you won't have to ask because you will know. That is when you will be more responsible. Now you will wait and feel safe with all this love around you, my lucky son!" Matteo raised those inquisitive eyebrows of his. He wondered who got to make up all these rules.

The question that begged attention wasn't how their lives together could get better, and we are not talking chocolate. The question to be answered was what could happen to make life events tumble down? (Stay tuned! Life can be so unpredictable. This little family had much to learn about life's twists and turns. The most important question wasn't about when changes would happen. It was what these changes would be.)

CHAPTER 2

W ITHIN A MONTH THE PACKING AND MOVING WOULD BEGIN. There were many preparations for this miraculous event. The children had not been taken on a tour of their new home prior to the upcoming move. Their imaginations were going wild. What would the apartment look like? What would their rooms look like? The month would not, could not, pass fast enough. There was not one person at their school who had not heard about this fantastic event. Izzy had to tell few as Matteo took this on as his contribution. His excitement could not be contained!

Matteo's latest question was, "So, when I am nine going on double digit, will we move again?" Maria, Carlos and Isabella were exhausted by his constant questioning. He needed to know everything and immediately! Maria decided that he had to write each question on a piece of paper and then they would select a time to answer them all.

His first question was, "When will you answer all the questions?"

"That," Izzy stated, "is a question. Write it down." As Maria anticipated, Matteo didn't like to slow down enough to write all those questions. After all, he was only six and it took effort. Some peace prevailed with this new addition to the family communication style. Maria was a very clever mother. She certainly knew her children.

A bigger home necessitated more "stuff" as Matteo was happy to demand. His mother always responded. "Yes, my love, we will need more beds and sheets but no more toys or electronics!"

"But" Matteo stated with eyes as big as saucers as he reflected on this need, "We will have more space for stuff like toys! Also, with Izzy going to be double digit we will need tablets and computers. When you get old like that you need technology. We are big kiddos now. Should we buy a computer or a tablet first?" The American dream was centered around technology for him. A phone for after-school check-ins was on the agenda for Isabella. With more responsibilities came more privileges.

Matteo thought that if he was able to gain these technological musts for his older sister, he might have a chance at sharing them. After all, he was her sweet little brother! She had always shared before. Why should that change? But change was, indeed, coming. He thought he liked change. Matteo was about to learn that not all changes were preferred.

The adventure had begun with a shopping spree at the local thrift store. They found a dinosaur bedroom set for 6-year-old Matteo. He was thrilled and ready to move on as his needs were met and he strongly demanded, "Enough here, now we…"

His mother Maria responded to his demands with quiet firmness, "NO! We are not done here." When she said it like that Matteo knew she was very serious. Disappointment showed on his little face.

Matteo was done furnishing his man cave with his immediate needs. He was done with essentials. He had other desires. However, done is done in his mother's book and they were not moving on. She was not done. She did, after all, have two children with needs! Matteo seemed to forget that Izzy had needs and desires, too!

Maria knew she would soon have to face Matteo's desire for technology as he had such an interest in every tablet, computer and device made. That would make his room complete in his thoughts, not hers! He would just have to wait until some of his sister's needs were met. Matteo's essential requirements were purchased. They were done with what he required to best make use of his own space! He was prepared to be bored with sisterly needs. He just didn't like it.

Isabella had needs, as well. Izzy could hardly contain her nine-year-old excitement as further exploration found a pink and purple bedroom set for a preteen girl. Someone had outgrown it but had cared for it with utmost responsibility. Izzy had been very patient and had known that she needed to wait until her brother's requirements were met or there would be no peace. She liked peace. How could something so wonderful be happening to them? She was a lucky girl. Life was so very good!

Would this, could this move happen more slowly? Isabella could almost taste the joy of this advancement. The American dream was within their reach. Their dreams were not large by most standards, but to these two children, this change was immense.

Izzy hoped that her wish for a kitten would be realized. She wanted a pet. She did not want goldfish or any other container pet. A dog would be too hard to manage with this busy family. She would wait until the right time to bring up the topic. Meanwhile she would use subliminal messages with displayed drawings on her door and walls. Books on cat topics would be carefully placed around their home.

Isabella understood what her parents had told her but not with great clarity. They had come into the United States with immigration visas. They had obtained work visas. Isabella felt that all was ok now. Their children, Isabella and Matteo had been born in the United States. The parental status for becoming citizens was going to be a problem for them in the near future. This fact was not one that occurred to her. She was only nine, after all. At this point her acceptance and happiness was intact with a family united. She was living the American dream.

The month absolutely crawled by. Then, it was time for the move. The very air seemed to be charged with excitement for Izzy and Matteo. The children were sent to school with the knowledge that when school was out, they were to walk to the new apartment. They had been walked, by their mother, from the school to the apartment building where their apartment waited, to prepare them for these walks on their own. Izzy could do it with her eyes closed.

They had begged to help with the move because, in their new titles as family assistants, it seemed imperative that the new roles and duties begin with the move. They accepted the change in their expectations when they heard that their parents had the day off and the help of colleagues with trucks! The children would go to school. Duties would begin after school. The words "after school" spun in their heads as they continued with plans for this new adventure. School seemed to last forever.

Finally, the bell rang, and they met at the door. Izzy grabbed Matteo's hand and dragged him out the door and toward home at a dead run. He was panting when they saw the apartment ahead. Then a miracle happened. Not only did he not have to be dragged but he flew beside her. They blasted into the building. Matteo looked at the elevator and Izzy pulled him toward the stairs. She puffed out, "Too slow! Run!" No one used the staircase so it was their own personal racetrack.

They raced up the stairs and then saw it! The door was wide open and a balloon was tied to the doorknob. As it bobbed, they read "WELCOME HOME!"

The walk to the door was slower and done in awe. They were dazed as they looked around. All their furniture was in place and it looked like home. They looked down the hall leading from the dining room. One door had a note taped on it. The note said, "NOPE, not yours! Move on!"

They walked slowly gazing at pictures hung on more walls that they hadn't had before. The next door had a note. "Matteo" it declared. Matteo opened the door and gasped. There was the bed like before but it had new linen on it. A nightstand held a dinosaur lamp. He had a little desk and chair. It was slightly used but just perfect. Next to the desk was a bookshelf fully stocked with books, new and old.

He turned and raced to his sister's room next door. The room had everything pink and purple. It was almost identical to her brother's but with bigger everything. Yes, that was how Matteo described it, "bigger everything." Her lamp was pink with crystals hanging from the shade. A large pink and white fluffy rug was beside the "new to them" bed. The bed even had a stuffed cat on it like a pillow.

CHAPTER *3*

SUNLIGHT TEMPTED BIG BROWN AND GOLD FLECKED EYES TO OPEN. The owner of those eyes didn't want to open them. She wanted a slow and much-loved approach to her newly found privacy. The alarm had not signaled the beginning of her first day of brother independence and she was not going to hurry this much longed for event. She would just lie here and feel the peace of avoiding a brother start the day. She was now in charge of her day's beginning.

She was a girl who needed the demand of visual and auditory input. They had just moved to this bigger apartment so both children could have his and her very own bedrooms. She had never thought this moment would happen.

No one had thought about setting the alarms. She was sure that she would never get tired of slowly waking and scanning this new and exciting initial independence from her little brother. This was her domain and hers alone. Could anything get any better? She tried to imagine how she could possibly improve this new chapter in her life. No possibilities came to her. Her exposure to the world had not included castles and riches so her present life was, though limited, still quite delicious and perfect. She was about to begin her weekend with new freedoms. She had wondered what her life without her invasive little brother would be like.

Her parents had friends whose children had outgrown bedroom sets. She slowly turned in circles to stop in front of the bureau with a mirror!

Her very own room had a mirror! The closet door stood open to reveal her clothes neatly hung on hangers! This was so very exciting.

When she thought nothing could get better, she remembered. The reason that alarms were not heard was because it was Saturday. She looked back at her pink and purple bed. Then she turned her gaze to her small bookcase with donated age-appropriate books. Her bed had a bedside table with a lamp on it. It was so fancy that Matteo would hate it. This was a good beginning to her new life!

One of the adults had left a book for her mother to read. She had noticed that eye catching book on the table by her mother's reading chair. Izzy had put that book on her little dresser. It had pictures of a white cat and a cute little boy. The title was "Chasing The Light". It took place in North Dakota. The author was Sandra Lee Brand.

She had started to read it last night even though her mother hadn't approved of it for her yet. There was a lost little boy in it. She fluffed her pillows into her favored position on her very own bed and put on her lamp. She hoped her mother would approve it for her as she just had to finish it. Izzy wanted to travel to other states one day and she really wanted to help little children like the lost boy. How could a child survive under those circumstances? Kiddos were supposed to have families to protect and love them. Now she had a new quest for her future. Just how many professions could she have?

She thought about the book. She had to read slowly to best understand it, but she was an above average reader. She looked at the cover and realized that it was the pictures of the white cat that had first caught her attention. To have a cat would be so perfect. It was all she needed to make her life Izzy perfect.

She really wanted a cat. She read all she could find about cats and was amazed that there were so many breeds to choose from as well as rescue cats with a variety of breed backgrounds. She wanted big, soft and gentle cats. She especially loved the long-haired varieties. Her mother had said, "Maybe one day. Maybe." Past maybes were coming fast and furious. She had her own room so maybe soon.

She would talk to her mother and get permission to continue to read

"Chasing The Light". She felt guilty for taking the book so she returned it to where she had found it.

She heard someone moving around outside of her room. She knew it was her mother as her father had already gone to work in that new used car of theirs! He often worked on Saturdays, so she knew it wasn't her father who was outside her very own door.

Her brother had been trying to come into her room to awaken her. Her mother had identified and restricted this newly found quest. Matteo was not used to being kept from his sister. Izzy could hear his protests. Maria wanted her daughter to have the full enjoyment of waking up with her new privacy rights firmly in place. This was almost perfect. She felt so much more grown up.

CHAPTER 4

Izzy climbed out of bed to find her jeans and T-shirt laid out for her by her mother. The clothes rested across the child sized rocker in her room. As she dressed, she combed her long burnished red hair to enhance the shine. Those brown and gold eyes danced as she looked in the mirror. She was positive that she looked even better in this new life. Her parents always told her that she was beautiful. Now she felt it.

She was ready and coming out of her room when she heard pounding on the entrance door. It certainly didn't sound like a friendly neighbor. Something made her cringe. Her brother ran to the door for this new surprise while her mother sternly called him away.

Maybe there was a new friend in the complex and maybe even on this very floor. Why should life change from fantastic and joyful to anything less. He really wanted to open the door to more excitement. It would be a boy with a tablet! He just knew it.

Maria opened the door to a red-faced elderly woman. The woman's eyes flashed with anger and the little family was immediately concerned. The woman wasted no time. "I am in the process of getting to know about you. We lead quiet lives on this floor!" She lambasted them with her raised and forceful tone. "Your child was running through the halls yesterday. I gave you the benefit of the moment, but today I can clearly hear his loud and raucous behavior. His sitter could not control him.

This is not acceptable. Any more of this type of disturbance will be reported!"

She hesitated to catch her breath, which allowed Maria to engage her in conversation. "I am so sorry if my son disturbed you. He was just excited about his new home. I will talk to him. He will respect your requirements for a peaceful home. The sitter is my daughter Isabella. We call her Izzy. We will talk to Matteo. He can apologize to you now. I am sure much of the noise came from us moving in. We want to be good neighbors. Matteo is right here."

The woman did not introduce herself but huffed, "We shall see. I hope his real sitter will have more control over him. I will not be responsible for any outcomes necessitated by any more problems. I do not need his apologies. His actions in the future will be indicative of his behaviors and those behaviors must change." With that last statement and a quick spin, she marched away while displaying her thoughts about this disruptive neighbor with a stiff back and quick dismissive steps to her apartment. She had had enough. Her domain would not accept such disrespectful behavior. She needed quiet and time to help her heal as much as one can when loss is massive.

Matteo watched. His big dark eyes were rimmed with tears. He had never been exposed to anyone who didn't like him or disapproved of him. He stared at the closed door. He had no idea of what to do to fix this. She didn't want him to apologize. What was he to do? The tears rolled down his round cheeks.

Isabella softly called to her anguished baby brother. He turned and ran to her where he was enveloped in her little arms. She crooned to him, "She just doesn't know how wonderful you really are. Don't cry, little brother. You are loved. Your joy is my joy but we will learn to express joy with greater peace and quiet. We will practice after breakfast, and I will help you. Does this make you feel better?" Izzy sounded just like her mother. Matteo sniffed and looked at his sister. She thought he was going to say "ok.", but he said, "I love love you Izzy Isabella! I do. I love you. But why does she hate me?"

Maria turned away so he would not see her tears. Maria wiped away those tears. The children would not understand tears from their mother. How had she been so lucky to have such special little imitations of Carlos and of herself? They would just have real butter and maple syrup on their pancakes. This was usually saved for special occasions. Perfect! It was the right time and the right reason!

Joy should not be punished but could and would be expressed with a bit more reserve. They were just children but not too young to learn respect for others. It would be a learning event with a reward.

Izzy whispered to her brother. "You know that Malo means nasty. That is what you and I will secretly call her." Matteo smiled. He was amused and felt a bit better. However, he understood that his behavior had caused the problem. New rules were not liked but necessary. This was a lesson learned for this vivacious little boy. He thought about his ideas to befriend that neighbor but knew his parents would not agree. He pondered and pondered until he smelled those promised pancakes. He walked, not ran, to the table, but he walked fast

Saturday was filled with discovery. Friends had given them out-grown toys and games. Matteo had discovered the small tv in his parents' room. He begged them to let him hook up the games left for him. He could hook them right to that tv and not disturb them on the bigger tv in the living room. Wouldn't that be the perfect solution? He never understood why his ideas didn't sound as good to others as they did to him. He would be quieter because he would be closer to the opposite wall from Malo. His Dad said books were even quieter!

Sunday was a trip to church and breakfast out. Wow! Life was going so very well! They went grocery shopping to have hurricane food available and for each of them to pick out a dessert for the week ahead. Then it was time to explore the new things and do their homework on their new desks. Izzy wondered who would have all these treasures once she outgrew them.

MORNING CAME AND THE CHILDREN WERE PREPARED FOR THEIR day at school. Izzy sat in her desk chair intent on the homework on her very own desk. She just had a bit to finish. Matteo was checking under his bed in case there was a tablet hidden there.

Carlos looked at his wife with pride very evident. The children hurried out with the intent to get to school and tell their friends about their weekend. Maria sent the children for the homework left in their rooms. Izzy had hers in hand but understood this was her mother's way of asking for a few minutes without little ears nearby.

This gave her time for a special quiet comment time with her husband. She turned to him and said, "I hope this ends now. The neighbor to our left told me that our neighbor, Matilda, had a special friend living here. Her health made it necessary for Genevieve and her husband, Melvin, to move near their children. I think Matilda is super sad and angry. She misses her friend. It is hard when you lose your husband and best friend. I often think of my parents. Life can be cruel.We must forgive Matilda and try to help her to not feel invaded by noisy happy children. Maybe we can find some way to make life more pleasant for her. However, for now we must make her feel less invaded. We will wait and watch. One day she will show us how to help her. I can only imagine how horrible it would be to lose my family and friends."

An apartment door opened and out popped two giggling elementary students. One first grader and one fourth grader were ready for school. The concerned parents stood in the doorway to wave goodbye to their kiddos. Maria and Carlos planned on following them but remain unseen. This would be the first and last time they could do this. The children must not see them. They must feel secure and trusted with their new power. It certainly was a power for them. This was especially true for Izzy. It was also very hard for the protective parents.

Matteo firmly grasped the hand of his big rule abiding sister. He whispered, "There is Malo's door." "Shhh." Izzy raised her eyebrows and Matteo got the message. He could be a good boy. Malo would see!!! He would make a card for her and charm her. It was a big task, but he was up for it! Mama had told him that Matilda was sad. That much sadness must make her crabby. Does great joy by others make sadness greater for people like Matilda? Maybe so. He could fix it. He had so much joy in his heart and he could share it!

He would begin to think of it right now. After all, his mama had always told him that he was her little charmer. "Just give me a chance Malo. Just give me a chance." he whispered. But, for now, school was waiting for him.

Izzy dropped Matteo off at his classroom. He gave her a hug and said, "See you after school, Izz! I love you. It's going to be pizza night!" As Matteo entered his classroom, he looked around for someone to tell about his new life. Who should he start with?

Izzy made her way to the office. She walked up to the counter displaying her most charming smile. "Hello Miss Angela. This is a note from my mom telling you that we have moved and the new address. We will be very close to the school. We have our own rooms. I will be ten soon and can walk with my brother to school and home. It is fun for me to bring you this note." This beautiful little girl beamed.

Angela was having a super busy day as news said that a hurricane was in the gulf. She had concerns but she couldn't help but smile. Her load had just been lightened by the joy emanating from this little girl.

Izzy had one major worry now. She had heard her parents talking about missing the deadline to remain workers in the United States. Izzy worried about her status and the status of her brother. She knew that her brother and she had been born in the United States. They were citizens. Wouldn't that make her parents citizens? How can kids be citizens and the parents not be, too? She had also understood that her parents did not want others to know before they were able to fix this frightening misstep. That is what her father had said. It was a misstep. That must be like a stumble. What did a stumble have to do with being a citizen?

The mind of a child can create frightening thoughts. This can be compounded when children are as intelligent and imaginative as these children. When the children cannot go to their parents for help this is quite a conundrum. (Now, dear reader, you have the beginning of understanding. This understanding explains where the lives of this family may go astray. Some of the premises are based on reality and some based on the wonderful and often, fearful, minds of children.)

These children have been living the lives that they believe to be perfect. They have friends and are loved by almost all (must not forget Malo) who get to know them. Matteo will always wish for more technology and try to figure out how to get it, and Isabella will always seek control and management within her realm.

CHAPTER 6

T HE CHILDREN CAME HOME FROM A WILD DAY AT SCHOOL. Hurricane Debbie was coming. School had gotten out early. Izzy clutched the shiny key which rested safely in her hand and hung suspended from around her neck on the shiny silver chain. She had felt so grown up when she and her mother picked it out.

Maria had taken her on a secret mission earlier in the week while Carlos and Matteo had gone to the Dollarama looking for tiny toy cars. Mama had said, "Ah, my little leader. You are in charge of the safety of your brother and yourself. This key will let you into our apartment if Daddy and I cannot be home to let you in. This could happen, but I trust you and Daddy trusts you. Now you can choose the chain to put that pink key on. You get to agree to this as it is a big grown-up thing to do and only ok if you agree."

Izzy looked up into the green eyes of her mother. Her mother's face was intent. She wanted this conversation to be ok with her nine-year-old daughter. It was a big ask. Life was becoming so complicated, and it was the fault of the parents. They were supposed to keep track of the requirements to stay in the United States and claim their dream, citizenship and the reacquisition of their true careers. They had gotten too busy and it had slipped away from their control. The thoughts about what could happen were frightening as she investigated the possibilities.

Maria had been a pharmacist and her husband had been a

businessman. He had managed a bank in Mexico. Upon arriving in the USA, Carlos began work at Sam's where being bilingual was an asset. Maria was also bilingual and soon found work at a Pharmacy as a clerk. They were not qualified to work in their true positions until they fulfilled requirements, but they were afraid to check on this as it would reveal that they had overshot their permissible time in the USA.

Quickly, they had begun building up their bank accounts to help to ensure the lives of their children. Citizenship and a return to their true careers was the ultimate quest. Soon Maria would have to explain this to her young Izzy. Maria knew she was putting a big responsibility on those tiny shoulders. She did not know that Izzy had already heard the conversations of their goals and carried the weight of their missions without the right to discuss it with them. She knew she shouldn't have invaded these secret conversations held by her parents.

Izzy watched her mother as those thoughts ran through her mind. Her mother was mentally far away planning and worrying, and Izzy was needed to help. She straightened her shoulders back into what she thought was a grownup stance. She had the same drive as her parents. Her responsibilities just started a bit too early. After all, she was not yet 10, the age of responsibility.

Izzy ran the silver chains through her fingers and picked the shiniest. She was ready to take command of the household until the parents were firmly in place to do so. She wondered about the tear as it slipped down the beautiful face of her mother…the mother she adored.

Izzy asked her mother, "Is this key because of the storm?" Her mother replied, "Partly, there may be a time when your Dad and I may not be home in time to let you in. I want you to know that you can get in safely. Your new phone will be used to let us know you are safely inside. It is only for that use for now. A key and a phone for my big responsible girl! I love you Izzzzz. They both laughed at this buzzing name adaptation.

I am sure your brother is counting the days until he is nine, almost ten. I have your new phone safely tucked into your dresser at home. He knows that it is yours alone…to be used responsibly."

CHAPTER 7

SINCE MARIA HAD GOTTEN OUT EARLY DUE TO THE IMPENDING hurricane she hurried to the elementary school to pick up her children. The threat was coming. They were as ready as they thought possible. The three rushed home. The children felt the anxiety of their mother and they tensed in response to it.

Reaching the apartment and opening the door brought Carlos into their view. This seemed to halt Izzy in place and brought a look of concern to the little face of her brother. This was new to him. He looked to those he trusted to keep his world in place and was puzzled as well as a bit frightened. First Mom had picked them up and now Dad was home when he should have been at work. Even big sister looked concerned. He slipped his hand into the hand of Izzy. She was his rock now and forever.

Debby rolled into the Tampa area as a tropical storm. Carlos and Maria closed the drapes on all the windows. They could hear but not see the chaos this storm created. Maria put music on and urged the children to dance and sing although she did keep a limit due to the sensitive neighbor. She also took this time to explain to them that their neighbor was alone and must be frightened so they must be considerate. Matteo kept his solution to himself. They had room for her in their hearts and in their home, but she would not want that, would she?

Matteo looked at his mother and dashed to the door. Carlos stopped him, "Whoa young man. Where do you think you are going. We are safe in this apartment as long as we stay together as a family."

"I am going next door to get Malo. She may want to be part of our family so she won't be afraid, and she will feel safe and loved. Please, Dad. I will be quick. I promise. No one should be lonely and afraid even though she does not like us yet! Maybe she will get to like us if we help her to not be afraid. Pleeeease!"

Carlos looked at his pleading son and felt, with wonderment, the boy's urgent need to be the friend of someone who truly did not love, or even like, them. That acceptance and yet caring had to be rewarded.

Carlos smiled at this little concerned being and said, "OK, my noisy one, I will go next door and check on her." When he saw the quick smile and raised eyebrows he added, "You may not stay at the open door and listen. I will come back and tell you what she says. This I do for her and for you, my sweet son. We will turn the music down and you can sing along with the music for background for her, but softly."

The deal had been struck and everyone understood their roles. Izzy turned the music down and Maria patted the couch area beside her for Matteo. This would assure her of the agreement between father and son to be secure. He would be still and wait with Mom because she was so close by.

Carlos opened the door with a big sigh. His thoughts were that they should leave this lady alone as that seemed to be her wish. However, he had a deal made. Carlos approached the neighbor's door with trepidation. He knocked softly and then a bit louder.

A lady opened the door with a determination that almost frightened him. He had not seen her before and found her to be an attractive woman somewhere in her sixties. Shiny silver white hair was drawn into a short knot of some sort behind her head. Her icy blue eyes looked at him, willing him to speak. After all, he was the one who came to her door.

Carlos bit his lower lip and started, "I am Carlos, your neighbor. My family thought you might like to come to our apartment to ride out this storm. We have a story telling event to start and treats. Do you like tea or some other beverage? We would love to know that you are safe with us. My son is particularly worried about you being alone, if indeed, you are."

Matilda, known by her friends as Mattie or Tillie, looked at him and he noticed the ice in those fierce eyes melt a bit, but just a bit, as she responded, "Please tell Matteo that I am fine. I am not afraid and have ridden out more storms than he is old. I appreciate your kindness but being alone in storms is not new to me. I appreciate, even more, the quiet he has chosen to give to me." With a slight lowering of her head, she backed up a step and firmly closed the door. The conversation ended with this declaration.

Carlos quietly returned to his family. Izzy was telling a story of a super cat who saved people without them even knowing it. She so wanted a kitten and had heard that the apartment allowed it. Now, she was at the end of the story and had the complete attention of her little brother. They would be safe. They had the protection of an imaginary feline, who was sent by God, her parents and maybe an imaginary grandmother. The cat she named Mystery had just swooped down and scared away the storm. Matteo applauded and turned to see that his Dad was back.

"Is she coming, Daddo?" Matteo smiled and displayed all the charm he possessed. His Dad could do anything! Carlos smiled and answered, "She is fine and feels safe. She has seen many storms and has protection only she knows. She did say she appreciated how quiet you have become.

Now, it is time for treats that are only storm treats and involve chocolate! Oh yeah, son, drop the Daddo. I am your Dad." Matteo responded, "Then I suppose that Daddio is not allowed." Carlos threw a pillow at his giggling son. The storm cannot stop the love of this family.

CHAPTER *8*

LIFE WENT ON WITH THE JOY OF A FAMILY LIVING THE DREAM. IZZY noted that her parents were later and later getting home from work and looked tired. She knew better than to ask them about it and didn't bring it to the attention of her oblivious brother. They dined in and rarely went out. Carlos and Maria even worked during the weekends. Usually, one or the other was home with them but never both at the same time.

It was almost always the job of this little girl to get home with her brother. She made sure the trips to and from school were done with songs, skipping and short stories begun on the trip to school and ended on the way home. He loved making up stories. Izzy thought he may grow up to be an author. It was his special job to make up stories without having to be slowed down by the struggle of writing.

Her brother was allowed to end some of the stories which always had superheroes in them. He was often the superhero himself. Izzy's desire to have a cat was drawn into the stories and the hero and heroine were Catgirl and Catkitten. Catgirl was a silver and black cat named Super Classi and Catkitten was a white Whirlwind named Super Jazzi and nicknamed Jazzamatazz.

Nothing was unusual when they arrived at the apartment with Matteo dragging behind but doing so quietly. That seemed like a big miracle to his sister. Something seemed just too quiet and even a bit

22

scary. She opened the door and Matteo raced past her with his new library book in his hands. He was one year ahead in reading and was intent upon raising that to two years like his sister.

There was a lamp on the kitchen table which was new as it was usually in the living room. It was turned on and leaned against it was an envelope with her name on it. She felt chills. She had lost her phone yesterday and felt that the envious Matteo had to be a part of that. She hadn't told her parents as she was sure that she would find it soon. She might have calls on it but didn't know how to find it. She was only 9 after all.

CHAPTER 9

I ZZY PICKED UP THE ENVELOPE. IT HAD HER NAME ON IT, ALRIGHT.
She pulled out the letter. It was long and that scared her even before
beginning to read it. If she didn't read it, could it happen? Could it be
real? Matteo would be wrapped up in his new book and not bother her
for fear she would tell their parents. He was supposed to give her space.
She looked at the end of the letter to find that it was from her mother.
The letter began:

To Our Amazing Daughter,

You may have noticed that we have been working very hard lately
and leaving you in charge. We saw that you were more than capable of
handling all that was necessary of you. We have confidence in you. That
allows us to do what is before us now. I am sorry that we must have this
grownup task for you to do.

Your Dad and I made a big and unforgivable mistake. We did not
keep track of the allowed time given to us in this great country. Someone
reported us to the authorities. I wrote this letter last week to put out for
you only if necessary and if you are reading it that means we have been
taken to Mexico. You know that Mexico was the country we came from
before seeking the opportunities offered by the USA and before you were
born to give you citizenship in the land of opportunity. You are citizens
but we are not.

We informed our friends that this might happen. If we were taken from you, they were to come and get you and you would stay with them until we were able to return. Your Dad works at Sam's with Alicia, and she and her husband face the same possibility that we do but it shouldn't happen to all of us. The agreement is that If your father does not go to work, Alicia knows what to do. Her husband is Marco, and their last name is Garcia. They will come to pick you and Matteo up from school. Their names are at the school to allow this. They have seen pictures of you and are willing to help us. I did not tell your school as our friends agreed to keep you at your school. You are both doing so well there. We want as little as possible to change for you.

We call them every afternoon. When they do not get the call, they will be there to get you. They are listed at your school so that they may pick you up. I do not want you to get lost in the legal work that happens with children whose parents have to return to their homeland.

We suspected this would happen, so we found a lawyer to help us. He will leave messages on your phone, so you know what is going on. His name is Mark Nelson. He will leave you his telephone number when he leaves you the message. He knows that all is well if you do not respond to him, and he is to concentrate on getting us back to the USA. We will make this happen as soon as we can.

We are going back to Mexico until this is fixed. We have built up money for you to have to help the Garcia's support you. It is in the box I put under your bed for your access. It is organized with binders for weekly use.

You are not alone my darling. The angels and the Garcia's will take care of you. You must convince Matteo that he is not to talk about this with anyone, so we do not lose you in the system that takes unattended children. This means that children who do not have parents to care for them will need to be taken to foster parents. You may not be able to be kept together and you may have to go to different schools. Our plan will allow you to not worry about this. I just want you to know why we are doing this.

They would not hurt you, but our plan will be better for you and easier for us to get you back. You will be ready for us to rejoin our family.

Please understand that it is our fault for not taking care of this and now we will be apart for a while, but we will be back. Your job is to be safe and make sure Matteo is safe. Do not scare him with this as he is too little. He loves, respects and honors you. All will be well.

We prepaid for six months so the apartment will always be there for you to go back to if you need to and we will return there. Please forgive us for our mistake. We will take care of this and be back. I promise. Soon we will be together and we will fix this forever and become citizens.

We love you.

Mommy and Daddy

CHAPTER *10*

Izzy went to check on Matteo. He was deeply involved in, "The Grinch Who Stole Christmas," and did not even look up. He was slowly and purposely sounding out each word and then rereading the sentence to make it "smooth". Izzy knew that meant he would read it to her later with more accuracy and pretend it was the first time he read those sentences to impress her. He always thought that he should be able to do everything she did. She would act surprised at his skill and praise him. He would want to read it to their parents.

She sat down quickly on the floor. Her legs felt wobbly. Is this what fear does to you? Just where were her parents and who took them? She would get a map and see how far away they were now. She stood slowly only to feel that weakness again.

She didn't have her phone with all the phone numbers placed in it by her mother. This would not be a problem if the Garcias came for them. Shouldn't they be here already? She had to plan. What if another hurricane came? She mused, "No, something so horrible could not happen for another year. Her mother said it was during Hurricane Season. My teacher said it was Fall and that was a season too soooo. Surely there couldn't be two seasons at one time."

She called Matteo to her, "Mr. Matteo, your table is ready. I have a menu for you. You may come and pick out something for dinner." Then she scribbled some food on a piece of paper and waited for the curious diner to arrive.

"What!?!?" he said already troubled.

"Mom and Dad won't be home for awhile. The Garcias will come for us but until they do, we will play grownups. Can you read the menu?" Izzy smiled with a mischievous demeanor on her face. Matteo studied her and then sat down.

"I will have the cheese and peanut butter crackers with the chicken noodle soup!" He ordered.

Izzy never allowed the smile to leave her face, "Very well, sir. You are also the entertainment and will read your new book to me." Matteo's face lit up and he ran for the book.

He was a little less excited about this game when it was time to go to bed but succumbed to his weariness and took his book to bed with him. She laid school clothes out for him and went to make their school lunches. She would use the money left on the table and under the bed until the Garcias came if she had to. She felt her stomach lurch. She sensed things were not right. Being almost 10 was something she had thought would be wonderful and eye opening. She would be almost grown up. Now she didn't want her birthday to come.

Matteo woke up in the morning and asked for his mother. Izzy said, "Mom and Dad had to go on a trip to learn how to make more money. They did that before when they went to the workshops. Remember? This time they had to go at the same time. If we are good and show how responsible we are there will be a special surprise. I will tell you when they are coming back. Don't tell anyone at school or we will have to pay for babysitters and there will be no money for surprises. Can you do it, big bro? Make me proud."

"Could it be a tablet? Maybe my own phone?" he questioned.

She smiled and said, "The bigger the secret we keep, the bigger the prize."

Matteo nodded his head as if that made sense and held out his pinkie finger for the pinkie finger pledge. This might even be fun. Little did they know.

CHAPTER 11

A WEEK PASSED WITH NO INFO FROM THE GARCIAS. IZZY LEFT their school with Matteo close beside her. There were warnings of a Hurricane. This Hurricane also had a name. If you dropped off the end of the name it was a better and more appropriate name for Helene. She wanted to tell Matteo but was not sure he would laugh. He didn't laugh as much as he used to.

She had told him that there was another change. Their parents had to go someplace else after the workshops. He kept asking for his parents and she would repeat that they were working very hard to fix a mistake made that sent them back to Mexico. They would be back and until they did, she was in charge. He surprised her by not wanting to be in charge. He no longer had to be told to be quiet.

She usually took him out for dinner after school. They had to be careful, but McDonalds was not expensive.

As usual, Matteo asked questions. "How come we have to eat French fries and hamburgers all the time?"

Izzy responded, "Because I am not allowed to use the stove much. It is also nice for you to play there. They have good activities for you. You seem to like it. You used to complain because Mom wouldn't take you there."

Matteo responded, "How come I can't have an ice cream shake? Mom used to let me." Izzy sighed. Being an adult was not fun like she had thought it would be.

"Go play and let me read." Books were her escape and allowed her to be entertained while keeping an eye on Matteo. Matteo must be worn out so he would be quiet when she brought him back to the apartment. She certainly wasn't going to have kids until she was triple digit. They did it in the Bible soooo.

Dinner and play were finally over. She gripped Matteo's hand firmly. He had been known to suddenly run when the apartment came into sight. He had his French fries in a bag and was unusually quiet. She held his hand even after they entered the building.

Malo was only a door away. They could not disclose that they were one wall or door away. Matteo's normal volume was loud enough to enrage the unhappy woman. Malo could not have a reason to come to their door to talk to her parents. They would be home alone and that could only mean trouble. She was only nine. Being almost 10 was not fun.

She suddenly felt sorry for Matteo. No wonder he was sadder now. He didn't have his mother or father or even his loving sweet sister. She was no longer the sweet loving big sister. She was the tired bossy mother replacement. He lost all the way around. He was beginning to realize this.

She looked around for the French fries but couldn't find them. She only hoped he had eaten them rather than saving them someplace like under his pillow.

They awaited a hurricane, and she couldn't even be comforted by anyone. She was the comforter. She put her hands on her face and quietly sobbed. Her hands came down and she wiped the tears. There were two reasons for this next move.

"Matteo, come to me." He slowly walked to her. His eyes were wide with apprehension. Concern was evident on his face where happy expectation should have been. "Let us clear off your dresser, now."

Oh no! Was she going to throw him out?

He begged, "No, I will be better! I promise." He covered his mouth with horror showing on his sweet face.

"Come brother." She turned and went into his room. He grasped his door to make it harder for her to throw him out.

She swiftly moved everything from his dresser to the floor to be dealt with later and turned to walk past him. She marched on into their parents' room. He gasped and held to the door with all his might.

Silence from him still allowed tears to roll down his face. Izzy picked up the smaller tv on the dresser in this room and marched past him right into his room. She placed it on his dresser and went back to get the remote.

"Come, little brother. This is now yours. Our allowances will go to pay for it for you. Yes, my allowance too. It won't have to go back to Mom's and Dad's room." She smiled, which gave her face an angelic aura. He walked slowly to her and she handed him the remote.

Tears rolled down his sweet round face as he turned it on with a quick look at her to gain understanding and reassurance. She walked over, kissed his cheeks and closed his door as she walked out.

She put on the big tv in the living room to learn more about the hurricane. Hurricane Helene was on her way. School had been cancelled. There were tear foods and drinks in the cupboards. Her friends had told her what they did in their homes and she planned to follow their examples.

There wasn't much in the refrigerator now as everyone told her to empty it. They told her refrigerators needed electricity to keep things cold so food would not spoil. She muttered, "Of course! Why didn't I think of that?" Surely McDonalds would be open. She had cereal and canned milk. Potato chips and crackers were within easy reach. Bottled water had been difficult, but she had managed to get it home with their little wagon.

Izzy looked around the apartment. What else would they need? She kept looking around the apartment, again and then again. There was a lot of what her mother called junk food, but her mother hadn't wanted her to use the oven so she had to improvise. She had used the microwave before so they could warm the soup and rice packets her mother had already stored.

They had canned meat that would be handy. She wanted to check on Malo but was afraid that they would be found to be parentless and not sure what would happen then. She didn't want to find out!

She had feared the police would show up if Malo had caused the loss of their parents. Could she be the one who told the police about them? She didn't know whom to be afraid of and whom, if anyone, to trust. How much more frightening would it be when she turned 10? She curled up on the floor and shook. Why hadn't their parents' friends come to pick them up as promised? She was sure her parents thought they were safe. She felt bad because they would be disappointed in her. She had to gain control.

As the day advanced the weather grew more dismal. Winds were picking up and the sky was grey. Dark clouds were appearing. Did they always look like that? She should have looked at clouds before. These looked scary.

Izzy looked at the bottles in a cupboard. She had asked her parents about these bottles. They told her they were for adults to help them relax after a long hard day. She certainly had the responsibilities of a grown-up.

The problem would be that Matteo would want some if she had some. Maybe after he was asleep. This was medicine for the problems grownups faced. She picked up one of the bottles and read the word "Merlot" and thought it didn't sound inviting.

She settled into the couch and watched the tv. The news scared her. Matteo was using his tv for his games and didn't know what was going on. She understood much of what they were saying but didn't believe that a constant, something that had always been there like electricity, would be affected. Unknown things were hitting the windows. Just when the loudest bang on the window was heard, the lights went out.

She heard Matteo whimper in fear. She knew she needed to make her way to his room. She immediately approached his door after picking up the flashlight her mom had left out on the counter. He was curled up with his back to the wall behind his bed. "Don't worry buddy", she crooned to him.

They played a guessing game. Izzy would ask him to think of an object and then she would have 20 questions to guess it. If she got it right, he would turn the flashlight on and highlight the object. This unique 20 questions game had him giggling while she worried. This too came to an end. They were able to fall asleep and then awoke the next morning with the electricity still off.

They could survive on their own without tv shows and games. Their meals could be eaten cold. Their parents had stocked the apartment with food due to the possibility of storms. They barely had time between work shifts to shop and prepare but they had done it. This was a great help to the nine year old in charge. She sat on the beaten fabric of the blue sofa. She gently rubbed the fabric her father had told her was "in" like the well worn torn jeans so many wore. She didn't understand why worn and torn was a good thing.

Izzy folded her hands and looked up. Three days had passed and they had remained in their apartment. The lights had not been on and she was getting tired of telling Matteo that he had to be especially good and quiet to earn the lights. He tried his best to follow her directions. He wondered where his fun sister had gone. He often thought of Malo.

With eyes closed and head bent she whispered, "Please, Jesus, give us light. We will be extra good and help anyone we can. But we are just kids and that is so hard to do and still be safe. You want us to obey our parents, and we have been doing our best. We must stay here and not let anyone notice we are alone." She was jolted out of her pleading by an energetic hug from her brother.

She opened her eyes to reprimand this little dynamo and realized she could see his beaming little face. He was doing his best to be quiet, "Izz, how did you do it? The lights are on. My tv came on! You are so powerful." Izzy sunk back against the sofa and began to cry. Her small body shook with relief and feelings she could not begin to understand.

For once in her short life, she could not control her feelings, but Izzy had never had such run ins with hurricanes. Maybe she had but her parents had handled it and she was only a little aware. She tried to push her mind back to the beginning of her life. When did she become aware of being alive for the first time? It was what she did when she couldn't sleep. Hummmph," she thought, "I just don't have the time or energy for this. Tomorrow! Tomorrow! I'll worry tomorrow. It's only a day away!"

CHAPTER 12

HELENE HAD COME AND GONE AND THEY WERE STILL ALIVE. Isabella had given up on the idea that the Garcias would come to help them. She did not know how to check on the couple and only knew that the pharmacy her mother worked at was close to the school. Today she had carefully devised a note and signed it with the carefully crafted signature of her mother.

After dropping off her brother in his room she took the note to the office and told them that her mother had brought them to school but was waiting for her outside. She had to take Izzy to a doctor's appointment. She would be back after lunch. Mom would take her out to lunch and then bring her back to school. Izzy scooted quickly away before the office marked it down and put the note away to be filed or . . .who knew? She was a kid, after all! This was one thing she was not responsible for so she wouldn't give the office ladies any help.

She went to tell her teacher and then slipped out the entry doors after being sure no one saw her. She ran and then walked to the pharmacy. She walked in and into the back area where she found the two pharmacists on duty. Fjona and Elisha both walked over to greet her. They had met her and seen her several times when she had gone in with her mother. "What are you doing here Izzy? We know your mom and dad are in Mexico but we haven't heard anything from her since she last called to update us." Fjona informed Izzy.

Izzy smiled her best smile and brought forth the well thought out information. She felt a sense of release because her Mom and Dad were ok. "We are staying with the Garcias who are friends. I had a doctors appointment so they took me. They couldn't find a parking place so they are driving around the block. Before she left, Mom wanted me to tell you that her attorney is Mark Nelson in case you could help."

"Oh yes", said Elisha. "He is my cousin and owes me a big favor so he is helping Maria and Carlos do what is necessary to come back legally. He is also helping them come back with the necessary steps to get their licenses here. We are all excited that she may be working with us as a pharmacist. We have been unable to fill the position so have to work overtime until Maria is able to join us. It sounds like it may be at least another month or so. When she calls again, I will tell her you stopped in."

Izzy felt weak in her knees with this news. "The Garcias lost their phone because they couldn't pay the bill but everything else is just fine. I think Matteo hid mine or was playing with it and we can't find it. That is ok though as I never used it. We can't have them at school. Maybe I can just check with you once in a while like I did today. I like to come and see you."

Both Fjona and Elisha came around the counter to hug her. Life had just taken a slight turn to the right, as in improvement! She slipped out of the pharmacy and ran to school where she checked herself in. Her legs were all wobbly from running and…worry. She added the worry of becoming a very skilled liar.

CHAPTER 13

ONE WEEK OUT AFTER THE OH SO SCARY HURRICANE HELENE and here comes another. The next week brought on a big scare with this Hurricane named Milton and it was rapidly becoming a Hurricane 5. With Matteo tucked away in his bedroom playing games and watching tv she became more anxious.

She had to keep Matteo calm and had no one to share her concerns. She thought of Malo. This lady could have been such a comfort but instead was part of the problem. It seemed as if Izzy was surrounded with dangers. It wasn't just Matteo she was worried about. her parents didn't even know the greater extent of trouble they added to her load. It was good they did not know.

She walked Matteo home and then tried to make their situation a fun game. She told him he was staying in a fancy hotel. She made a menu with various soup choices or chips and a tuna sandwich. This time he helped with the menu.

The news only became worse. They are on the 3rd floor and she hears that this does not mean that they are safe. She doesn't understand the hurricane paths and why some areas are in worse places. She doesn't know about her home. Was this a bad area to be in when the storm hit? What can she do? She knows that her parents want them to stay in Florida as they are citizens. Her parents will come back but when?

They had this week off from school to get ready. She had taken Matteo with her to a nearby Publix store. Someone had given them a wagon when they moved, and it had been used as a toy box and a place to put their books. Now they used this wagon to go get groceries.

She had listened to the smart people on the tv say that they would probably not have electricity. They would need food that did not require electricity to prepare. She even let Matteo pick out some breakfast and protein bars. She knew milk was not a good idea. She carefully counted out her money. She had added her allowance savings to make it go further. She had emptied her piggy bank even though it was not yet needed. This would be a math lesson for her brother.

Since it was Wednesday morning and the storm was supposed to settle in with more vengeance, she allowed Matteo to pick out four candy bars. He had insisted upon five because he wanted to share one. It made no sense to her but cutting them all in half would allow them to keep track of time with a half every hour or maybe 2. Protein bars and water in plastic bottles, bananas and oranges were added to the stack she had collected on her own when she had called in sick while Matteo had stayed in school. She even had two flashlights from the dollar tree.

When returning to the apartment building, she let them use the elevator. The elevator made noises that may upset their neighbor, so they rarely used it. Matteo lagged behind as usual now. He was quiet so he won this new reward. They were ready to face this new danger...maybe.

Matteo immediately went to his room and turned on the tv and his games. She had told him to be sure to plug in a tablet to charge. A friend had given it to Matteo when a new one came his way. She heard the little tv go on so she turned on the tv in the living room and watched and listened to the news.

She was scared, so very very scared. Suddenly she realized that Matteo had come into the room and then immediately left. She instantly became concerned that he may have heard the oh so terrifying news. She turned the sound down and went to look for him. He may need comfort.

He was not anywhere she looked. Then she remembered the coveted candy bars and headed to the kitchen. He was not there but only 4 candy bars remained. He had been here. He had to be hiding with that forbidden treat. What a time for him to have become naughty.

She scanned all the hiding spots. She had closed the curtains so he couldn't see the storm beginning to show nature's rage. She quickly went outside the door into the hall. He wasn't there. She raced down the stairs and checked each hall as she went from floor to floor. Outside? Oh, please no! The door could have locked him out. She carried the key around her neck on her silver chain.

The rain had started and the wind was blowing everything past her. She stepped out and called his name. A lady approached her as she hurried by. The lady said, "Did you lose someone, dear? The storm is kicking in now and you must get inside. I will call the police for you." Izzy felt her heart fly to her mouth.

She gasped, "No, I remember now he is with his friend next door. Silly me. Thank you so much." Then she turned to open the door. The lady raced off.

She ran up the stairs and retraced her steps. She fully expected him to be back in the apartment. She listened at every door as she passed for her brother's voice. Maybe someone had taken him in. The lights went out.

Izzy fell to her knees and couldn't stop the sob. She dropped to all four as she gasped for air. Light came across the threshold of the door next to her and her face froze in open-mouthed fear. There stood Malo. Malo held a lantern. Just then a little head peeked around the lovely silver haired lady. Matteo!

Izzy thought nothing could be worse. She had found out from the pharmacists that someone had turned her parents into the authorities. She had harbored this fact deep in her heart. Had Matteo just handed them over to the person who might have been that unkind being? After all, she seemed to hate them. She was so shocked and so worn out that she dropped to a sitting position.

"Well," Malo stated, "It seems you have a problem. You have lost your brother. I am sure your parents or the Garcias are very worried.

Will they be here soon to stay with you? Matteo said that is the case so he has been staying with me until someone came.

I have been getting little presents on my doormat for several weeks. I even got an entire candy bar today. I have stones painted with hearts, french fries, notes and small cars and toys. It appears that I have an admirer. Today, I was going out to check my mailbox when I caught the culprit." She stared intently at the culprit's keeper, also known as Izzy.

Izzy touched her forehead to the hall carpet and thought fast. She raised her head slowly and said "I am so sorry. Sometimes our babysitter comes here to pick us up and Matteo must have sneaked out while we waited. I am so sorry. I will ask Marco and Alicia Garcia to come earlier. Sometimes we just have a regular sitter here. Matteo seems to have a fondness for you but I will keep him away."

"Oh no, you won't." said Malo, "You may call me Mrs. Green. Right now, my culprit, whom I have discovered is not a culprit after all, is having cookies and milk. He has promised to read a book to me. I am holding him to his promise. You may join us or you may take a break. You look like you need a break. He has been very good and quiet which is why I never caught him delivering his notes and gifts."

At this point she looked at Isabella in an inquiring manner and Izzy replied, "I do need a break. The sitters will ring from below and I will come for Matteo then unless he comes home before. Please send him home after he has read his book to you. He is only 6 so it takes longer. I thank you so very very much." She quickly turned to go to her apartment and then heard the click of the door. It was then that Izzy let the tears flow. Maybe it was time for that fancy anxiety reliever called Merlot.

Then, she slowly closed the door to her apartment. Yes, she now thought of it as her apartment. She quietly thought to herself, "When will I be able to drive that car parked in our parking area. I should have grown after all this adult stuff I have been doing. Can I reach the pedals and see out the window? Do I need to wash it? No, Hurricane Milton may do that for me. How long should she wait until she went for Matteo?"

What other mandatory tasks do grownups like her have? Are others more pleasant? What should she make for them to eat? One more night of cereal would be ok. Matteo seemed so relaxed. He had a grownup to talk to and answer his endless questions. The grownup could be an even harder hurdle for them. Why did Matteo try to do the things he did?

She didn't realize she had fallen asleep until she heard the door open and shut with Matteo pushing a dish at her, "I already ate with Mrs. Green (no more Malo) and she sent this home for you in case you wanted some. We don't have to eat with the babysitter. I don't like to lie to her. You do it from now on." The mac and cheese had big pieces of chicken in it and tasted like Heaven. Soon they would pretend the sitter came to sit with them.

CHAPTER *14*

THEY WERE TUCKED INTO THEIR ROOMS WHEN HURRICANE Milton Struck. Izzy was on alert even while sleeping. She sat up at the first bang, sprang out of bed and ran to close the curtains and maybe mute the volume of some of the terror called Milton.

She stopped in front of the window in rapt awe at what she saw. The sky was a soft gold and a strike of lightning went straight down. Never had she seen such lightning. The once blue sky turned the most beautiful shade of green. She couldn't take her eyes off it. She felt a wave of fear followed by an awe she had never felt before.

A small hand fit into hers. "Matteo, we should not feel fear. Only God could send such a thing of beauty." A tiny voice answered, "Wow. This is better than fireworks. Ok. What do we do?" Izzy sighed, as sanity returned to her and the circumstances demanded action. She didn't feel like crying. She felt like sinking to the floor and hiding her head.

"Well, little brother, we will move away from the window. Even great beauty can be dangerous and I do not know the message carried by this." She turned to switch on the lights to discover they were not working.

Izzy reached for the flashlights and said, "Come, we will go into your room and sit on the bed. I have some ghost stories to start for you. I will create a problem and you may bring out your super beings to save the people in danger." The fun began and then Matteo cocked his head to listen.

He leaped from the bed and ran to the door. When he opened the door two very wet creatures rushed in. They were light in color and the light coming from the window was reflected from their silver and white coats. Izzy quickly grabbed towels and rubbed these beautiful cats with fabulous long silky fur dry. Her prayers had been answered. That was, at least, one of them.

Someone must have opened the door to get in and the cats saw their opportunity. They wore harnesses that were torn and barely hanging on. Izzy used the flashlights to read the silver circles hanging from the harnesses as she removed them. "The silver and black cat must be named Classi." she said. Matteo handed the other circle to Izzy. The name said, Jazzi. "Well named." Izzy said.

The silver and black striped cat gazed at the children with eyes that turned from green to gold. They then turned to the pure white cat who displayed her very blue eyes to the children. They were also God's work of art. Izzy felt that a state of calm had come in with these beautiful feline beings. They were calm and so was she.

Matteo and Izzy opened a can of tuna fish and shredded newspaper for an improvised litter pan made from a dish pan. Matteo purred in time to the kitty girls and Izzy felt the calm she had not felt in what seemed forever, continue even through the worst hurricane in 100 years.

That night passed quietly and peacefully with each child curled up with a special visitor. The worst hurricane in 100 years raged on but did not touch the conscious levels of these two little lost lambs. Their guardians kept their vigil.

CHAPTER *15*

MORNING CAME AND IZZY WOKE UP FIRST. SHE SAT UP TO FIND Matteo to her right. They had fallen asleep on the rug in her room. One cat slept on either side of these two like furry buffers from a challenging world. The room was not dark and she was surprised to discover that they had slept through the devastation she would see outside. She felt the continued calm. "Well girls," she said as their names probably mean both were girls.

She had no way of finding out if there was school because the electricity was out. The storm hit on Wednesday so she knew they would not have school the rest of the week. A week out from school would mean makeup time. Her teacher had told them of this possibility. Her plan was to check on Monday if possible.

Izzy would leave Matteo at home with the girls watching him. Do cats babysit? Well, these two would. She would look for signs from their owners. She would warn Matteo that if he made any noise or left the apartment the cats would have to go. This scared him and gave him a purpose for his best behavior.

Izzy slipped out of the apartment and saw trees and poles down. She looked for anyone looking and calling for the cats. She thought they were very irresponsible for letting the girls out. She wanted to find the owners as they must feel desperate. At least, she should want to find them.

She walked on to the local grocery store. They were well stocked with regular food that required no heating. She was getting tired of their choices. McDonalds was closed. She didn't want to spend much on restaurant food. She really didn't know if they would do pickup in a small mom and pop restaurant. Would they let a kid pick up food-even a kid with money? No sense taking a chance. They couldn't take the chance of letting anyone find out they were on their own.

As she walked, she noticed a man who seemed to be following her. When he saw she had noticed him he said, "Hey little girl. I lost my home in the Hurricane. Are you on an errand for your parents? Why are you alone?" Izzy quickly looked around and moved closer to her school with the chain link fence. There were bushes on both sides.

The man said, "Do you have any money? I am hungry." He moved quickly towards her. Just then two balls of puffed-up fur came out of the bushes. They looked big and very angry. The man cursed and said, "DOGS!" He turned and ran just as a police car pulled up and stopped him. Izzy couldn't stick around even though she wanted to help the police with this man. She ran and two cats ran beside her. She looked back and saw the police putting the man in their car even though he didn't want to go with them.

She stopped to catch her breath and looked for the cats. They were gone. She could only hope that Matteo was playing with his games and not following the girls. She stopped in the grocery store and bought some cat food and treats as well as a small bag of litter and three candy bars. This was all she could carry. She could always bring the cat items back if the cats didn't follow her home.

She got home with some stops to adjust her packages. She used the elevator because of her burden and quietly walked to her door after dropping off one of the candy bars on the neighbor's door mat. She looked at the door before she used her key to find it was ajar! Oh oh! She walked in and was greeted by a boy and two cats!

"Matteo! The door was open!" scolded Izzy.

Matteo was distressed. "I was playing with my games and the cats were napping. When I looked for them, they were gone and the door was a little open. I couldn't find them. I left the door a little open so they could come back in!" She saw he had been crying. Mysteries!!! She wanted to rename them Mystery and Mystique, but they refused to answer to any name other than Classi and Jazzi.

Matteo looked sad. "What now?" she inquired while managing her voice to stay calm with him. "You are Izzy and they are Classi and Jazzi. I want to be Mazzeo or Masseo so I match."

Then the lights came on! She felt a bit of relief. Would they stay on? Would there be another hurricane? She felt the warm silky fur rub against her legs and she sank to the floor. Her tears were gently licked away until she no longer felt the need for tears. They agreed on the new nicknames of Mats and he could call them Jazz and Class. The names would not stick but for now Matteo's crisis was averted.

CHAPTER *16*

"**H**EY GIRLS!" CALLED IZZY, "I GOT SOMETHING FOR YOU. LET us feed you real kitty food. She put down the cans and let them pick one. Amazing, they did! At least Classi did and Jazzi simply watched her do the work.

Izzy would get them more choices and maybe even make them a menu. Yes, this she would do. She got a piece of paper and dipped her finger in their rapidly disappearing food. Then she touched the paper with the cat food choice. Now she had the first item on the cats' menu.

Matteo watched with interest. He went to their cupboard and got out the tuna fish. He gave them a bit more and then repeated the finger dip and entry on the menu. He was all smiles.

What about our menu? "No finger dips" Izzy declared. "because we can read. You now read well enough to use a menu like regular people, at least the menus with pictures. Soon you will be able to write well enough, too. OK! Let us work on our menu!" and they did. Matteo was busy drawing pictures for the cats on their menus. His fish was pretty good, but his chicken, Oh my! Peace reigned.

Matteo went to his room to play his video game. The cats trailed him like they knew where the true supervision was needed. Izzy decided that she would have to come up with some chores for Matteo for his good and hers.

The vacuuming put her in a world of her own. She then began to survey the apartment and put away everything that was breakable. She didn't know how busy cats were. She would put it all in her bedroom closet so she would know where it was. Maybe she would even find the phone. She would go through all her pockets again. Maybe the closet floor!

What a day! No one was around to tell her what to watch so she found out that the Hallmark Christmas stories had begun. Kids at school told her that they were begging their parents to put up a Christmas tree. She knew they had a small one in the closet that was locked on the main floor. Everyone had a lockable closet in the back area of the apartment building. She didn't have that key.

She went downstairs to the storage area to try the door just in case. It was firmly locked. She looked at an adult getting something out of the storage area and wanted to ask him a question. She wouldn't let herself ask any question, "Would Mexico let her parents come back? Would the United States let them come back now that that the USA knew they didn't follow all the rules?

Who could she ask who would know and then not figure out that there were kids here without parents right in front of them?" The questions remained unanswered as she raced upstairs to tend to Matteo and the cat girls.

Everyone was there so she thought she would listen to the news. It scared her as they talked about another hurricane to be named Rafael. It sounded like all would be fine. November was the last month for hurricanes.

"OH! The tv said that school was back on. Matteo would be happy to see his best friend, Richie!" she murmured to herself. Then she remembered! Richie's mother had talked to Maria. They wanted Matteo to have a weekend sleepover.

They would pick him up from school on Friday so he had to take clothes with him. The school knew about this weekend treat for both boys. Matteo would return to school on Monday with Ritchie. That would be best for all the grownups due to their work schedules. It certainly was best for her too as she could not reach those gas and brake pedals to be able to handle transportation for Matteo.

This wasn't supposed to happen until after this week of school. She had some planning to do and notes to write. The first note would have to be delivered to Richie's teacher on Monday. She would also be there to be sure the boys were successfully launched on this special weekend.

CHAPTER 17

IT WAS SATURDAY AND MATTEO NEEDED A GETAWAY FROM THE APART-ment. Next weekend he would be with Richie and entertainment would not be her responsibility but that was a week away. She had hoped she could get the tree out but that just wasn't to be.

She went in to check on him and he was awake playing under the covers with the girls. He would move his feet or hands and they would pounce. He was giggling hysterically. When had he learned to giggle so quietly that even she had not heard him? She suspected that Mrs. Green may know they were alone. She had to be especially quiet and well behaved. Matteo was always the problem.

Did she dare take Matteo with her to see Fjona and Elisha? She couldn't take the chance of continuing to go from school to see them. No kid needed to see a doctor that much and then the nurse at school may decide to get involved. If she didn't do it during the school day, there was Matteo. He had to go along. She had to chance it.

"Matteo," she said. "You are a good actor. We have to go see Mom's friends where she works. You must be quiet and pretend you are a little shy. Can you do it?" Matteo cocked his head and pouted a bit, "You like to talk for me anyway so what is new?" "Oh oh," thought Izzy, "Matteo is being a little sassy."

Nonetheless, they walked to the pharmacy. The lady at the counter picking up something turned to look at them. There was recognition.

They knew her and she knew them. Fjona immediately noticed them and said, "Good news you two. Hi Matteo!" Matteo cocked his head and gave her his best smile. He said nothing.

Mrs. Green stated, "Well, hello neighbor. Does your mother work here?" Elisha, who had been waiting on Mrs. Green answered her! "The pharmacy is holding her old job for her and we hope she will be back soon!"

Mrs. Green beamed and said, "Oh yes, she must be the one I haven't seen in here for awhile. What a small world."

The two pharmacists turned to her, "Is there anything else you need?"

Mrs. Green replied, "Oh no, I must get back. I am on a mission, you see."

After Mrs. Green left Izzy looked up at Elisha, "You have heard from Mom?"

"Yes. She is uncomfortable that she is unable to talk to the Garcias but likes that you check in here. She knows they are trying not to be involved with the authorities for personal reasons. Mark is working hard for your parents. I assume the Garcias are keeping up with what they need to do for themselves. Your parents want us to not bring attention to them. They are comfortable if you report in here occasionally. I asked your mom about putting us on your pickup list at school as a backup. She sent me a note for them. Are you ok with that?"

Izzy breathed a sigh of relief. "Oh yes! Please. Matteo is going to spend a weekend with a friend. Can I give her your name to call in case of an emergency?" In response the two pharmacists came around the desk to hug Matteo and Izzy. They handed Izzy their calling cards to give to the school office and Richie's parents.

That was a relief as she thought that she may need some backup as the school figured things out or became suspicious. After all, she was only a kid and couldn't keep up this pretense forever by herself. Soon someone might figure it out and then the government would take them. She had been lying and she was getting too good at it. Did they have kid jails? Things would be better now. Was Mrs. Green figuring things out?

CHAPTER *18*

THEY LEFT IN A HURRY. SHE SAW THE SCARY MAN WAS BACK ON HIS corner. She went in the opposite direction and saw that McDonalds was open. Many trucks were parked there. They were the men fixing all the downed poles and trees. They slid into McDonalds and found the play area open and it was evident that Matteo was starving. He wanted to buy an apple pie dessert for later. It was a small concession. He must be growing as he often wanted to buy a little snack for later and she never saw him eat them, but they were gone. So be it.

They hurried home and unlocked the door. The cats were gone again. Just how did they do that? She stopped and gasped. In the living room was a decorated Christmas tree. It was lit and under it was a new litter pan, and cat food as well as catnip toys. Did Santa really exist? She also found out that you can really cry for joy. She had heard that grownups did that. Did that mean she was a grownup now? She didn't want to be a grown up. She didn't even want to be ten. She would just refuse to turn ten. Crying when you were happy was just not something she wanted to ever do. However, she did.

Tomorrow is Sunday. When they woke up it would be Sunday. They had not been going to church but she put it on the tv. It was not the same but it would have to do because she had not found the car keys yet. She had to keep praying to keep ahead of all those adult tasks she didn't want. She had been in such a hurry to be responsible and do grownup things. You should never wish for something you did not understand.

What if Mark couldn't get her parents back? They had broken a law about how to be a USA citizen. They had to get licenses to do the work they wanted to do…what they were good at. Being a grownup was so very hard.

The week went fast and now the school had someone (pharmacists) they could call if they needed to. It wasn't fair to make Elisha and Fjona do this extra job. Now Izzy had to feel guilty, too!

Friday came and Matteo was so very ready. He was nervous as he had never stayed away from home before. School was over and she stopped on the sidewalk to see that Matteo was picked up. She had packed clothes for him and watched him swinging his little pack of clothes as they waited.

He had wanted to pack for himself but that ended when she saw him trying to pack the girls. It was hard enough to keep track of Matteo and the girls without the cats escaping from the apartment building. The car arrived and what a car! She could recognize a fancy car when she saw one. Both boys were so very excited. This had gone so smoothly that she was worried.

Then she saw the scary man standing across the road from the school. Matteo was safely away and now she had to do the same for herself. While she kept her eyes on the man she hurried away. She was so occupied with keeping an eye on the red-haired man that she ran into someone. She turned to look up into the face of Mrs. Green.

"Oh!" gasped Izzy, "I am so sorry! I…I…am going to meet the Garcias after dropping off Matteo to go stay with his friends." Izzy was very nervous and turned red.

"I am fine." Stated Mrs. Green. "You don't look so fine. Do you need help?"

"Ummm, no. I just wanted to make sure that Matteo is on his way and not be late to see the Garcias. I must hurry now. I want to leave food for the girls before I leave. They will be late and we will come and go from the apartment as they like to shop at Bealls and I can make sure the girls are ok."

Mrs. Green smiled. "Don't worry as they dine with me as well."

Izzy backed up, then turned and ran. This time she did not look back.

CHAPTER 19

F JONA AND ELISHA WENT OUT FOR DINNER. THEY HAD BEEN PHAR-
macists for only three years and were very skilled with personalities
plus. They were friends and roommates and had gotten involved in the
problems as Maria had told them. They discussed the situation as they
dined.

Fjona said, "I just feel that there is something different about this
situation. We promised Maria that we would keep an eye on the kids if
they appeared and they did. I have always thought that Izzy was mature
beyond her years but she seems a bit stressed. The parents don't have
contact with them, but the Garcias must be in the same situation if they
do not want to meet us. I think they may be hiding. from the authorities
but have no evidence. I know Maria has told us that they may not want
to be visible. I am pretty sure I know why but…"

Elisha responded, "I agree with you. Izzy was so very happy when
I told her that we would put our names in their files at school for con-
tact in case of an emergency. Maria was arranging what she could from
Mexico with Mark's help. The school has been very accommodating."

Fjona smiled in reflection of a conversation she had with Mark.
"Mark was very pleased when I told him that we would be willing to
sponsor Maria and Carlos. I think I am becoming very fond of those
two little lost children. It must be tough to not have your parents nearby.
Mark is handling the sponsorship of their parents as we talk.

Elisha reflected, "When we found out that Mrs. Green was a neighbor to those dear children, I wanted to talk to her and find out if the Garcias were living there with the children or in their own area. Maria said she had left it up to them just so the kids could stay in their present school."

Fjona added, "I know Mrs. Green used to be a welfare worker for the state and she was very competent. She even took the foster care training and took in wards of the state at one time. When she lost her husband, she retired and we didn't see much of her anymore. Her husband was the love of her life. She had sold her home and moved into an apartment. If Maria agrees I would like to talk to her, but I don't know how much we should interfere with what is going on. I would feel better if I knew more about the Garcia couple. I guess that for now we will watch and wait."

The conversation moved on to their social life as well as work related features. These young women wanted to help the world one crisis at a time. They were well on their way to doing just that! For now, they were happy to help Maria and her little family. They would be there for them at any time and for any reason.

It was time for dessert and a celebration as their boss had just agreed to wait for Maria to return before hiring another pharmacist if these two competent and well-liked ladies could cover. It was an easy thing for their manager to agree to as he liked Maria and knew the customers also felt the same way. These three ladies were well admired.

They called the waiter and ordered a hot chocolate dessert to share. After all, they didn't want to gain weight. With the hours they were putting in at work that wasn't even a possibility. They just hoped the little family could be reunited by Christmas. That was their toast done with glasses of red wine to go with chocolate dessert. Life was good.

CHAPTER *20*

AFTER IZZY SAW THE JOYOUS BOYS GET INTO THE CAR, SHE TURNED and felt the weight of the world partially lifted. She ranged from relief to fear for him. He was in good hands but they were not her hands.

She slowly walked to the little grocery store. Everything was so handy from this new apartment of theirs. She bought a loaf of bread and more of those rice packets you could just put in the microwave. Her favorite was the coconut jasmine. She would watch another Hallmark movie and have microwave popcorn. Her mind flicked to that Merlot but she didn't know how to open it. Her little bag included a coke to go with the popcorn.

As she walked, she saw the scary man slumped against a tree. He was not too clean and looked so very alone. She eased up to him and put the bag with the bread and coke beside him.

She turned and went back to the store. She told them she had forgotten something and bought another loaf of bread, a candy bar and some chips. As she left the store, she moved the bread to one of the other bags. As she passed the sleeping man she put the new bag beside him, too.

She kept looking over her shoulder as she walked away. He slept on. She sighed with relief. Maybe he was just hungry and lonely. He was too scary to be her friend, but it didn't mean she couldn't help him a bit.

She took the elevator again. When she got to the door, she noticed Classi and Jazzi lounging in front of her door. They couldn't get in when

56

the door was locked. She opened the door and the three of them went in to watch Hallmark. But first, she took one of the bags of jasmine rice and quietly set it on the doormat of Mrs. Green. She wasn't so bad. They were ladies on their own. Maybe she was watching Hallmark, too.

She set out the cans of food and watched Classi make her choice. She opened the salmon and put down fresh water. Jazzi watched and then jumped onto the counter to drink the water drops left running for her. The girls and Izzy had learned a few things about each other. Classi calmly touched the water in her water dish to get it to move before licking it off her paw and then from the dish.

Izzy took her jasmine rice from the microwave and plugged in the tree before curling up on the couch. These three were in for the evening. Izzy couldn't believe it, but she missed her little brother.

She smiled as she imagined how free the little boy must feel to play with noise and joy! She couldn't invite Richie to their apartment but maybe the boys would be so delightful together that Matteo would be invited out again. He had even taken the book he found under the tree, the Grinch was featured, of course.

CHAPTER *21*

RICHIE COULD HARDLY WAIT TO DRAG MATTEO TO HIS ROOM. THE toys in that room almost made Matteo speechless…almost. "Wow! This is amazing! Are there any toys left for Santa to hand out?" Richie laughed and hugged his friend. Matteo was his hero. Richie was young for a first grader and small for his age. The other kids called him a kindergartner and wouldn't play with him. Richie cried easily and was a nervous little boy.

The boys were having a really good time when Richie's mom came in to get them for mac and cheese with hotdogs, Richie's favorite. Matteo was afraid to talk. He didn't want to be taken away from his sister or his whole family if that was even possible.

Richie's mother, Amy asked Matteo, "You are a great friend for Richie. He says you protect him and tell the other kids that Richie is a great friend and that you won't be their friend if Richie is not included. Why do you do that?"

Matteo thought about his answer to make sure it would be safe and then replied, "I like those other kids and they are missing out on a great friend. Richie is a great friend. He is kind and helpful.

He cries and they don't like it, but he is crying because they don't want to play with him. We have signals so Richie knows he doesn't need to cry. Now the kids like him and he doesn't cry anymore. He is not a baby, but he cares too much. That is what my sister says and she is very smart. She was right about Richie. I am not his only friend now."

Amy and Bob looked at Matteo with amazement. "How old is your sister? She is very smart and so are you. Your parents must be wonderful people."

Oh oh...the "parents" word. Should Matteo not say anything or just think about it first. "My parents work very hard. They want to help people. We have family meetings and talk about all these things. I want to be like them when I grow up. Izzy is nine going on ten and must help me a lot because sometimes I don't always make the right choices. I don't know how she knows so much...maybe when I am nine going on ten, I will too."

Bob said, "Well, our Richie made the right choice in choosing you for a friend. You seem to know more than most six-year-olds. Your parents have done a great job teaching you values."

Matteo thought carefully and then said, "Do you want my parents to teach you how they help us? They can't right now. I can tell you when they can...just not now. Izzy says I talk too much. Can we talk about how to play all his video games? I don't know how and he doesn't either!"

Both parents laughed. "You are definitely an honest six-year-old boy. OK. Let us play video games. Who do you think should do the dishes?" asked Bob.

Matteo said, "Well, probably not us. We are on vacation. Maybe we could toss a coin. That is what Izzy and I do. Usually, Izzy says that I am a good sport and helps me. Maybe we could all do it!"

Amy added, "Bob and I will do them now. You guys can do them tomorrow. Of course, we are going out tomorrow so this is a very good deal for you!" Bob doubled over in laughter and the boys ran off.

CHAPTER 22

THE SCARY MAN ON THE STREET OPENED HIS EYES AND LOOKED AT the bags beside him. He had lost his home in the hurricane and all his possessions. He had lost his job before that. His wife had taken their two children and left. He had been drinking and was super depressed. She had had enough and didn't want her children to see the fall of their father. She was with her parents...he thought.

He hadn't meant to scare the little girl, but he was so hungry and she was the only person he had seen all day. She was walking and everyone else had been driving. He shouldn't have done it. He had scared her and then tried to talk to her to apologize. That scared her more and then those little dogs ran at him. The police rolled up right at that time and had turned around to stop him. After checking his story, he was dropped off with information on where to go for help.

He was allowed to talk to a contractor who was looking for help with recovery work. They were going to meet later in the day. The scary man named David was going to walk to his bank to see if his wife had left him any money. He would rent a room and clean up. He did have a suitcase with the clothes he had been able to save from his flooded home.

When he lost his job, he lost his temper and drank excessively. He woke to find his family gone and a note saying to not contact them until he was sober and in control. They had fled from him and then the hurricane that was coming. He was told to leave his house and he left with a suitcase of clothes and went to a shelter.

He remembered hearing someone say he needed to be scared straight. Mission accomplished. The bank would decide his next move.

He had scared this little girl and he felt so ashamed. Now she had brought him food. This was a sign for him. He said a little prayer that the bank had some money. These were all signs. He had a mission.

He went to a service station, cleaned up and went to meet the contractor who met him at a local restaurant and hired him on the spot. He wanted a drink but stopped for coffee at a church that was offering free lunch to those affected by the hurricane.

The next feat was to find the car he had left somewhere. He was close to the shelter where he had sought and found safety. The car was there and the keys were in the ignition.

The bank was his last chance to make this all work. He walked in saying a small prayer. He promised that if he could have this resource, he would become the man his wife had married and maybe win her back. Everything had come so easily for him and then…

The bank was the last ultimate chance he needed. The smile he got when he entered was followed by the information he sought. His wife had taken only what they had needed. She planned to get to her parents and return to her profession as a teacher. She was leaving him a chance…a hope. This wouldn't have happened without that sweet and kind little girl. He hoped she had forgiven him.

CHAPTER 23

I ZZY CAME UP THE STAIRS. HER JOB WAS TO HIDE KNOWING THE Garcias were not coming. She didn't know what had happened to them and that scared her. She had watched a news program she found on the big tv. It was not really a news program but she didn't know what else to call it. It was about people who vanish and no one ever finds them. It scared her.

Surely the Garcias would have gotten information to someone who could have helped her in this quest she knew she was too young to handle. She was to keep an eye on Matteo and not let anyone know that she and Matteo are on their own. She had heard about street kids. She knew she shouldn't feel sorry for herself because she had watched a program that had street kids in it. They had to do things to survive that she did not understand. They were in other countries and here. It scared her. They, however, did not have an apartment.

So many things ran through her head now that Matteo was tucked safely away. She had watched the scary man after she dropped the food. It seemed to revive him. Maybe he was just hungry. Was he lost like Izzy and Matteo but with no parents to help him? His hair was red and his eyes so very blue. She would recognize him if she ever saw him again. She wanted to know he was ok but also never wanted to see him again.

It sure was easier when she had only been a kid. What if he had figured out that she was all alone with no parents? Would he look for her or just tell the police about her when they picked him up? Would Mrs. Green report them? She was smart and could have turned them in even though she kind of liked them now. She didn't want to think that Mrs. Green would do that to them.

She heard steps behind her and it scared her. She reached the second floor and opened the door to that floor. She hid behind the door which was partially open so she could see who was behind her.

Two fluffy heads appear above the top step to be followed by the furry bodies of Classi and Jazzi. They couldn't have made those walking sounds. For one thing, they wore no shoes and then their feet were little and quiet on those furry paws. The steps kept coming.

She looked from side to side. She couldn't see a weapon. It was too late to run. The walker could hear her running and follow her. Milk was not a weapon. There were the Little Debbies but they wouldn't be any more help. Maybe if she threw them the walker would take them and leave her alone. That didn't make any sense. How had the walker gotten by the front door of the apartments?

Then there was the voice, "Well Izzy, why are you hiding behind the door. The cats are pointing you out. What are you afraid of?" Classi plurrrted and Jazzi did a loud Yarroww. They had pointed her out! The rest of Mrs. Green came up the stairs. "Perfect timing," she said, "I just bought a pizza. It is too big for me and I really don't like warmed up pizza. Are you here alone?"

CHAPTER 24

"Ummm. Sort of. Just for a little while. Matteo is having a sleepover with a friend and I am going to do some schoolwork while I wait for the sitters. I like to do my homework. I want to be able to go to college one day...like my parents. I think I would like to be a doctor for little kids."

"Well then, you must plan on making yourself a sandwich or something. Why don't you help me out by eating some of this pizza? The girls are going to spend the evening with me since you won't be home later. I think they would like it, too."

Izzy could feel the fatigue. She could smell the pizza. What would it hurt? Mrs. Green would be so much better than tv. She smiled and relaxed and said, "Well, if I could help you by eating pizza, OK."

The four walked up to the third floor and into Mrs. Green's apartment. "I will put a note on the door for the Garcias. They have their own key and want to drop off something for Matteo."

Mrs. Green gave her a piece of paper and a pencil. Tape was there for her, too. Izzy went to her apartment and put the note on her door. She then took the groceries in as well. She opened the Little Debbies and took out two packages...dessert, you know.

Mrs. Green had left the door open for her, but she gave two hesitant knocks anyway. Mrs. Green waved her in. The table had placemats and silverware. Izzy looked alarmed and Mrs. Green understood. "Izzy, I always eat my pizza with my fingers but thought you might use silverware. It is your choice." Izzy responded, "I like to use my fingers, too. I use paper napkins to wipe my fingers but I see you use cloth." Mrs. Green whisked off the cloth and put out jolly Thanksgiving paper napkins. "How happy and homey this looks! That was a good idea, Izzy." Izzy beamed.

She had done something right! She always wanted to please and felt she had done just that. The pizza sauce would stain those beautiful cloth napkins. When she was older, she would use fancy plates and cloth napkins like Mrs. Green but for now she was only a kid, wasn't she? She just didn't know anymore. What she did know was that she wanted to please Mrs. Green. Stains made her remember Matteo. He was a champion with stains…making them, not avoiding them. Laundry was on the schedule for this weekend.

After their pizza party, Izzy said she had to go home and wait for the Garcias. She prepared to leave and then looked at Mrs. Green. She so wanted to feel that someone else was in charge and she missed her parents' hugs. She looked away and then glanced back and lowered her head. Mrs. Green got the message. It was something she was good at. Her career had evolved around her intuitive nature and she had been, and was, darned good at it.

"Izzy," she began as she walked over to her and put an arm around her. "Would you mind a hug? I am really good at them. Someday I will tell you who taught me to be even better at them. I really like you. You are truly an extraordinary little girl." Izzy turned into the arms of Mrs. Green and a serene moment passed between them. This time the tears were not on the cheeks of the child. Izzy was aglow with that hug and smiled as she hadn't for weeks.

Mrs. Green was going to get involved in the story next door. She just couldn't stop herself. She felt a purpose and a need in these children. After all, this is what she understood so well. She had served a public now left behind…until now. Would this be a good thing or an unveiling that could be painful for the two little residents next door? Mrs. Green represented the very thing Matteo and Izzy feared the most.

CHAPTER **25**

ATTEO AND IZZY WERE SPENDING A WEEKEND APART. EVEN SO, their thoughts often went to each other. Matteo was worried about who was taking care of his sister. He had no way to communicate with her and didn't dare ask Richie's parents for help. Part of his conscious thoughts were on the marvelous life he saw in this household. He knew he had to be careful of what he said but careful was not a word Matteo fully understood.

Morning came and Bob opened their door with the declaration that breakfast was served. Bob and Amy were doing their best to let the boys enjoy each other with limited adult supervision. It was unusual to see their son so free, happy and independent. This is how a little boy of six was supposed to behave.

Richie arose and began to jump on the bed. Matteo was horrified and showed it. He could break the bed! Bob rushed in and caught Richie in midair. He spun him around and placed him on the floor. "Would you like me to catch you, too?" asked Bob.

"Oh no! Izzy would tell me not to break the bed. We don't do this at home. Anyway, Izzy is too little to catch me. I could break her!"

Bob raised his eyebrows in thought. Why would his little sister have so much control? "How old is your sister?" inquired Amy who was peeking in to take part in the morning routine.

"She is nine and she is the boss of me even though I am better at doing things right now. Izzy says she is very proud of me." Amy couldn't help but ask, "What do your parents say about what you two do?"

Oh no! He had said something wrong. His face turned red and tears appeared in his eyes. "We have a sitter in the morning. She is making breakfast. Izzy and I each have our own rooms now and it is her job to wake me up. She has the alarm clock and has big sister duties." Matteo saw these two adults looking at him as if deep in thought. He had to do something fast but Izzy always told him to think first. "Izzy walks me to school and home and is in charge until the Garcias come. They are our big people sitters. They are in training to be parents."

Bob thought, "It is none of our business if the children are ok and they seem healthy and happy." He was to repeat this thought as soon as the children were so very busy eating. Omelets and cinnamon toast with orange juice was on the menu. They smiled at the enthusiastic attack their picky eater son had in imitation of his little friend. They were both hungry and happy.

Amy quietly replied, "Let us keep an eye on these two children." However, she knew full well they would not have the time with their court schedules. They were both trial attorneys. Nonetheless, they had the day with these two and conversations could lend to more concern or relief in outcomes. It was now time for Matteo to protect or disclose their lives. This was simply the way of Matteo's life.

Amy thought that Matteo was old for his age or, perhaps, their son was too protected. Matteo was a good friend for their Richie. He was so considerate of the feelings of the adults as well as Richie.

Amy looked at her husband and said, "Neither of us really knows as much as we should about child development. The counselor at school told us that Richie was young for first grade and somewhat immature. Perhaps that is what we are seeing or sensing." Bob nodded and then smiled as Matteo had Richie laughing so hard he had to sit down. Matteo had picked up Richie's new book about the Grinch and was reading with the proficiency of a much older child.

Amy thought, maybe she should talk to the boys' teacher about having Matteo tested for Gifted. Then she concluded that she would talk to Matteo's mother and suggest it. There was a PTA meeting coming up and that may be the perfect time. Certainly Matteo's mother would be there.

Bob called Matteo. "Do you know what we do? We are attorneys. Do you know what we do as attorneys?"

Matteo was pleased to show his knowledge. "Oh yes. We have one of you. Izzy says his name is Mark Nelson. Do you know him? He is very important and helps people."

There, yet again, was Izzy's name as the one with family knowledge and control. Interesting. These thoughts floated through Bob's mind.

"Yes, we do!" He is very good at his job and a very nice person. Bob made a mental note to talk to Mark about this unusual family. "What do your parents do?" Bob continued.

"My mom works at a drug store. She helps the people who give you medicine when you need it. She has two friends who are farma some-things. She is going to do that again one day. My dad used to work in a bank. Now he works at Sam's. He will work in a bank one day again. We will celebrate when that happens. Izzy says it will be a big celebration. She said we would have flags."

Amy and Bob look at each other. How much can you really learn from a six-year-old? His perception of life and living is interesting, but how factual? Nonetheless he understands more than Richie. Does he know more than normal or do they just not keep Richie informed. Maybe they need to do family meetings like Matteo's family does. Maybe they should let Izzy lead them. It sounds like Izzy would be very capable of the job.

CHAPTER 26

ELISHA AND FJONA WERE BUSY AT WORK. THESE SIX-DAY WEEKS were getting tiresome. They decided to give Mark a call and ask him about the progress. He wouldn't tell them. He never did! Maybe they could go out for lunch with him tomorrow.

There was talk about a temporary clerk to help cover for Maria. After all, they hoped Maria would come back as a pharmacist and they would need a helper anyway. This would be the perfect way to try someone out.

They were also hoping that Izzy and Matteo would come to visit. They really wish they would bring the Garcias with them but they had figured out that the couple probably were also not legally in the states and wanted to keep a low profile.

They wanted to tell Izzy that they had offered to sponsor Maria and Carlos. Mark had said this would be a great help. They wanted to invite the foursome to their apartment for Thanksgiving. They had not had anyone over since they moved into this job and left their families behind.

Elisha had moved from Minnesota and wanted to go home for the holidays. The temporary should be able to handle the paper part of their job and the manager, himself a pharmacist, had said that they could both go for a one week break as they had been working so hard. He had also hired another pharmacist as business was booming and it would take a while before Maria could be fully functional according to Mark.

Fjona decided to ask Izzy if she would bring the Garcias to their apartment for Thanksgiving. It wasn't that far away and it would be fun for Elisha and her to make a special dinner.

The school had notified Elisha and Fjona that there would be a special program on Monday and that both Izzy and Matteo would be reading special stories they had written. Elisha had contacted Mrs. Green and she would join them there.

Each grade would have two students read their special writings. This had been a different event as the children had an afternoon to write totally on their own. They had been submitting writings done at home for the last two weeks. Then the chosen few from these writings had gone to the library and while supervised by the librarian they had written their final draft. From these writings the final winners had been chosen.

Two groups of four children from each grade level had made backgrounds for the stories. The two pharmacists had bought special presents for the Martinez children. Izzy Martinez and Matteo Martinez would be presented with certificates for their home displays. It was a great honor and the writings along with others from each grade would be sent to the mayor for yet another award. Teachers and students were thrilled.

Monday was the big day and the classes had been canceled for the presentations so there would be a large audience. Elisha was going to record it for Maria and Carlos. The event would be after everyone's lunch and there was even talk about a television crew. This was a big event for all the schools in Pinellas County.

CHAPTER 27

S UNDAY AND ANOTHER DAY ON HER OWN. IZZY HAD BEEN PRACTIC-
ing her presentation for Monday. Her heart ached that her parents
would not be there. This was a big event every year. In the past years her
parents had helped her to write the presentation. She had always gotten
special mention but this year she had won.

This may be a problem if her parents had to be there for any other
competitions. There was some thought that all the winners would be
brought up for a district wide competition. It would be announced at
the end of this event on Monday. Parents or guardians would have to be
there. Why did this have to be so very hard?

Maybe Elisha and Fjona could be their guardians. What did you
have to do to be a guardian? She would google this after school. She
should talk to them and the attorney, Mark Nelson.

Enough! Izzy scolded herself. She had to practice this speech. She
wanted to present it with as little reading as possible. They were told that
they could do it either way. Maybe she could just mess it up and then she
wouldn't have to worry about a final competition. BUT! what if Matteo
won? That would be worse because he couldn't go alone and she would
have to stay in school. For sure, she couldn't go with him. OK. She had
to win, just in case.

What happens to children without parents? Mom called them unattended. Would they go to some kind of foster home? She had seen this

on a movie with a little girl named Orphan Annie. That hadn't been real but why would they make a movie that wasn't real or at least based on real things. Maybe they would be sent to Mexico. They couldn't do that because they were not citizens there. What had her parents been thinking!?! These thoughts raced through her mind in whirlwind fashion. She had been doing ok so far. She just had to go on playing the game.

Now, she thought the next step was to win this contest. She would do her best. It had been enough so far. What could go wrong?

CHAPTER 28

M ONDAY MORNING FINALLY ARRIVED, AND IZZY SNEAKED OUT of the apartment early. She ran all the way to school while watching for that red haired man. He was nowhere to be seen. Maybe someone had hired him, and he had a job. Maybe the food she had given him helped him to have the energy he needed to do something about his life. Izzy wondered what had happened to him to make him look so lost and alone. She hadn't really seen him since then, at least not lately. When she prayed at night, she prayed for him. He had seemed crazy and yet something about him made her sad and not as scared as she probably should be.

She went to the front of the school to watch for Matteo. She had hoped being able to see if his face would tell her how his weekend had gone. Maybe he would have time to talk to her. It had seemed too quiet and lonely without him. She had loved getting to know Mrs. Green better. She sensed a loneliness akin to her own in this lovely lady. Her smile lit the room much as her frown made things dark.

The car arrived and the doors swung open. Two little boys jumped out arm in arm. Amy called to them. They turned back for their back-packs and lunch boxes. They were laughing and hugging each other. Both boys were hugged by Amy before she drove off. Then Izzy felt so much emotion that she could not tell if it was joy or grief. They had been delivered rested, happy and ready for the big day ahead.

Izzy stepped away from the corner of the building she had hidden behind. The boys were running to the door and Matteo saw her. He screamed her name and ran to her with arms out. Life was ok in her world again.

"Did you have a good time?" She asked.

"Oh yes!" both boys answered. "I made something for you." Matteo chirped in excitement. "Me too!" added Richie.

She gave both a hug and said, "Well, when do I get it?" "Soon but not now!" both boys breathlessly added. The bell rang and the two boys turned and ran for their rooms. Izzy had planned on walking them to their room but they had simply charged off together. She turned and went to her class. THE DAY had begun. It would go slowly until 1:00. Richie's mom, Amy was happy sad about the big event. All the other kids would have someone special there for them. When they performed, who would cheer for the Martinez kiddos?

CHAPTER 29

IT WAS TIME! THE STUDENTS CHOSEN FOR THIS HONOR WERE IN FRONT of the gymnasium on chairs placed on the stage. Each grade level performed a musical opening guided by their music teacher and monitored by their teachers. They had already heard their winning classmates' performances last week. It had been anticipated that the gym would be crowded even without the classes so they were taken back to their rooms by their teachers. The gymnasium was packed and chairs had been added to the aisles.

The students were waving to their special guests. Izzy looked down at her feet. She had on the shoes bought for Sunday school. She didn't want to look up and then have no one to wave at. She thought she heard her name but continued to look down. Her best friend next to her nudged her and said, "Look, my parents are waving at us!"

Izzy obediently looked up and couldn't believe what she saw. There in the front row applauding, beaming and waving were Elisha, Fjona and Mrs. Green. All three were waving flags with her name and Matteo's names on them. Further in the audience were Amy and Bob and they were calling her name and the name of her brother. They were rewarded for their love with the broadest smile Izzy could deliver. She saw Matteo throwing kisses and joined him in his enthusiasm. Then, the music teacher asked for quiet and the crowd complied.

The kindergarten student was adorable and only missed half of his presentation as he couldn't maintain attention and kept stopping to call to his parents. Nonetheless the crowd applauded and both scared and thrilled him. The music teacher, Mrs. Jones, had to go on stage and carry him away to join his class in their fun celebration in his room. He definitely liked his fame.

Matteo had been called from his seat in the front and stood as he was introduced. The speeches were about what each student was thankful for and why. Matteo's speech covered his family, his friends, special treats and, especially, his sister. This brought oohs and aahs from the audience. It was quite eloquent for a little boy. He ended the talk by turning to face his sister and extend his arm for her to stand. Then he threw her kisses before turning and delivering kisses to the entire audience. He was radiant. The audience was enthralled. The sponsors for this event, the Kiwanis Club, also seated on the stage, and they rose to applaud him.

This presentation was followed by second grade, third grade and finally fourth grade. Izzy wore a pretty new red, white and blue dress. She had found this hanging sideways in her closet when she went to select something this morning. Her teacher had pulled up part of her long hair with a special matching ribbon that had been dropped off for this by a special gift giver.

She deliberately looked at her special guests in the front row. The front row had been reserved for donors so Izzy knew what they had done to get those seats. Tears formed behind those long lashes but were wiped away before she began.

"My name is Isabella Maria Martinez and I am nine years old. This speech had been hard for me to write as I have been gifted with very special people in my life.

My parents loved and worked so hard for my brother and me to enjoy what this special country represents for all of us. My parents came to the United States so their children could be born here and be citizens. I am not going to tell you what country they came from as I want you to believe it was the country your family came from. Each and every one of you was given this gift. I love this country for what it offered to my parents and my brother and me.

I am thankful for my little brother who amazes me every day. He loves all who he meets with as much energy as only Matteo has. He returns this love to me in everything he does and says, even when I often shake my head at what he really says. I love you, Matteo.

Those special people in the front row have taken Matteo and I into their hearts and made us feel safe while my parents fight to return to this, their chosen country.

You don't even have to stop to think of the complications two children like my brother and I bring to you. You welcome and love us.

We love you back. That is what this country is about. It is about all of you who sit out there and celebrate your children or kiddoes as Matteo calls us. I thank God for all of you and this country as you have made it, the welcoming home it is.

With that said, I hug you...all of you." Izzy made a big circle with her arms to illustrate this hug and then her tears fell. The audience stood and clapped as one. This was the most one-minded action shown by the audience. They had chosen their winner.

The Kiwanis representative group whispered amongst themselves. Plans were being made to check out this story. How could they help? The television crew, sent by the local television station to catch this beginning for the ultimate Pinellas County contest for the best "Children's Thankful Presentation", did so with enthusiasm.

What had Izzy done? She would soon find out. She had spoken from her heart and may have made more of a problem for these two lost little souls. Would anyone hear the hidden message of their plight?

CHAPTER *30*

FJONA, ELISHA AND MRS. GREEN LOOKED AT EACH OTHER WITH questions foremost in their minds. Discussion in the front row would be moved to a place of coffee and speculation later. This discussion would center on the fact that none of them had ever met the Garcia couple. What did this mean?

For now, the speeches went on to cover family, games, technology, teachers and pets as reasons for thankfulness. Select parent groups applauded and cheered their children but there were no more complete audience demonstrations.

The music teacher, counselor and administrators continued to move the performance along. The children were given the choice to return to their rooms for celebration or an early exit for family celebration. It was decided that they would do both. First, the celebration in their rooms followed by an hour early dismissal for performers who wanted to go home for more celebration.

Mrs. Green, Elisha and Fjona went across the street to the City Center for coffee and conversation. They had suspicions and were concerned that the television exposure and Kiwanis' attention would reveal even more. They were amazed that none of them had seen the elusive Garcia couple. Could it be that the children were on their own?

It didn't seem possible that these two children could manage such a

d pick the kiddos up while Mrs. Green

deception. Their parents had thought ahead and gotten help from their friends.

Everyone had trusted information from Maria and Carlos. Mark had been keeping in touch with the parents and guiding them through what was necessary to bring them home. What more was needed?

Mrs. Green had been involved in the state process for placement of the lost children left behind by parents sent back to their countries of origin. This involved situations where the children were born in the USA. Preferably, the children would be reunited with their parents in the USA. This was what Carlos and Maria wanted, and they had passed these desires to their children. She decided to check on her status with the government and with foster programs as needed. She may have to step in to help.

The young pharmacists said they thought that they should see if they could sponsor and care for the children here in the USA if needed. The problem was if these two young adults would move in different directions. It was a big responsibility they had not felt they could do… maybe for a while, but even the Garcias may not be qualified for this responsibility. Where had they been for the big moment just experienced by Izzy and Matteo?

The presentation just given by Izzy demonstrated the importance of being able to follow through with the desires of the children and their parents. For now, these thoughts had to be discussed with Mark and Maria and then…who knew?

It was time for them to pick up Izzy and Matteo from school for their early out. Fjona and Elisha would pick the kiddos up while Mrs. Green proceeded to work on their quest for knowledge.

CHAPTER 31

E LISHA WENT INTO THE SCHOOL TO PICK UP THE TWO CELEBRANTS while Fjona waited in the car. They were taking them out to get ice-cream sundaes. This was a great time to celebrate. Izzy was so impressed that they had come to observe her. Izzy had made the pharmacists and Mrs. Green the subjects she spoke about and they were very touched.

Mrs. Green went home to call acquaintances still in the business of unattended juveniles. She would put out feelers and hope her old acquaintances would respond with updates.

She would wait to meet with Elisah and Fjona until after they attempted to meet the Garcias, talk to Mark, Carlos and Maria. It was time to get this figured out before something negative would happen to these two little angels.

Mrs. Green had conflicted emotions. Would her assistance create a problem for this little family? It was entirely possible that the non-existence of the Garcias could throw a wrench in the process. If she finds out something like this, she would be obligated to turn them in, wouldn't she?

She had been the foster parent for many children. Most of them had been in her custody when her husband was alive and she was younger. They had seen these children grow up and now see her as their mother, but more had been turned back to their parents. She was now 67 and the right age for retirement. Fjona and Elisha were so young to get involved. If the task went astray, they would be wounded for life as well as the two children.

Time would reveal more complications for all involved with this situation. Hopefully, Mark would be able to resolve the issues coming forward. He was their first resort. He was a young attorney and doing all this pro bono. He was on the rise and work was increasing for him.

The Martinez wanted to keep money available for Izzy and Matteo but offered to pay now and then later with payments. Mark had attended the school event and left with distinct dedication to the situation. Perhaps it could be a political gain for him later in his career.

For now, Mrs. Green sat thinking about the entire process. E and F (as she called them now much to their amusement), had decided that they were too fond of Mrs. Green to call her Mrs. Green. They had started off calling her Matilda and then Elisha started calling her Tillie. It had been what her dear husband had called her. She had the choice of smiling or crying…she picked laughing and so it was decided. She was now officially Tillie.

She decided to take the children out for pizza tonight to celebrate. She had the feeling that Izzy would win the speech contest. The crowd had shown their choice and the Kiwanis judges had been leaning in that direction. She had noticed the television crew move in for close ups. Izzy was so emotionally involved in her speech that she did not see them. She was saying it just for the small group in the front row.

Tillie felt that darned tear she had been holding back roll down her cheek. She hadn't planned to get involved. Just then the front door was pushed open and Classi and Jazzi strolled over to remove that tear and demand a treat. Their job was going well.

CHAPTER *32*

C LASSI AND JAZZI RAN TO THE DOOR AND, STANDING TALL, HIT the door knob. Their combined weight swung the door open and they rushed out. "Aha!" Tillie addressed those beautiful animal angels, "That is how you do it."

She heard these cats chirping and trilling their greeting to the children. Tillie joined the group. The children were aglow with their day. Without thinking, Matteo ran to her with his arms out. Tillie knelt and accepted the hug with a big smile. Izzy felt a smile of relief but couldn't stop it. Tillie looked at Izzy and returned it. Tillie then stated, "I want you to reach the Garcias and ask them if you go out with me for pizza. Tell them that I will stay with you overnight, so they don't need to come to get you so late. If they agree, come over and we will watch an early Christmas movie until it is time to go. Does that sound ok to the two of you?"

Matteo accepted immediately but Izzy said, "I am sure they will appreciate that as they work late." Matteo looked at her with eyebrows raised and then suddenly, understanding flooded his face. He smiled and nodded in agreement. This young man should never play poker.

Izzy and Matteo went into their apartment. Izzy realized that they were not supposed to be able to call them without phones. She folded up a piece of paper and put it in an envelope. Then she ran downstairs and put the note on the door in case anyone checked. Before she went down, she stopped to tell Tillie she was going to put the note on the door for the Garcias.

Tillie watched this through a slit in the door. They went back into their apartment to put their supplies away. Izzy was going to help Matteo with his homework and then they would be over. Tillie went down in the elevator and opened the note left on the door. Nothing was in the note and then she knew. "Oh, those poor little ones." She thought.

Matteo rushed over to Tillie's and was beaming. Tillie asked, "Did you hear from the Garcias?" Matteo quit smiling and dropped his eyes to the floor, "Izzy said I should tell you that she left a note on the door downstairs and went down to check to see if they had taken it. That is a sign they will let us go."

Just then Izzy came upstairs and said, "I ran into them when I went down and they are happy to have the night off." Izzy looked stressed.

Again, Tillie thought, "Those poor little ones." Out loud she said, "Ok my little neighbors, let us go! We can have two if we can't decide on the same kind. We will have enough for leftovers tomorrow. Maybe the Garcias will check on you in the morning. Ask them if you can stay with me for the week and next weekend. Then we can celebrate every day. I think you will win the contest. You are both amazing. I will see you get to school on Monday. If they agree, they won't have to come for you until a week from today."

CHAPTER 33

Amazing! The Garcias did get the message and agreed. Izzy and Matteo rushed up the stairs with Classi and Jazzi in close pursuit. They knocked on Tillie's door and were greeted with open arms. Tillie thought, "This week I won't have to worry about them. They will be with me." The cats strutted in like the royalty they probably were.

Tillie looked at the beautiful regal beings and thought that she probably should notify the apartment caretakers and pay any deposit necessary. But they came and went at their will and their rightful owners might arrive at any time to claim them. That is, if they allow themselves to be claimed.

She had posted information on the girls everywhere appropriate and even in newspapers. She hadn't put their pictures in as anyone claiming them would have to present proof in the form of pictures and she didn't want scammers to see their worth and attempt to claim them.

But, most importantly, these cats seemed to own them and not the other way around. Maybe their owners let them roam and they returned to their rightful home when not with their adopted homes. Those owners didn't deserve these cats because there were so many dangers in the real outside world. Maybe the owners were within this building. That would make sense and make this all ok. In any case, these cats could not be contained by anyone. They were free spirits and liked it that way.

In any case, Tillie invited Matteo and Izzy in to see the two spare bedrooms in her apartment. The first was done in cream and blue. Her late husband's car collection was artistically arranged on high shelves. Matteo was mesmerized. "Could I maybe sleep in here?" Matteo whispered. Izzy immediately corrected her infatuated little brother with "Matteo, these cars are not toys. You can look but not touch. We can sleep in our own rooms when it is time for bed."

Tillie gently corrected with, "I would love for us to have a real sleep over or I could come to your apartment. I would not want you to be alone. Which would you prefer? Wait, let me show you the other room."

When they entered the next room Izzy felt a calmness. It was a soft white and seafoam green. It was very feminine with shelves of collector dolls. This room was larger than the first room. This must be the luxury apartment on the floor. The far corner had a white desk with file cabinets arranged around the oversized desk. It was a dream world for a businesswoman not afraid to enjoy her feminine side. Izzy quietly murmured, "Well, it would be like a vacation to stay here. I wouldn't even want to leave to go to school. Do these rooms really have their own music system and tv?"

Tillie laughed and said, "What you see is what you get. So, should I assume you will be my guests for this week?" "I could be a kid again." Whispered Izzy. She didn't intend for anyone to hear but Tillie heard and understood. She had her work cut out for her.

"During your stay I will make your lunches for school. I could also arrange for you to eat in the cafeteria if you like. What do you think?" Izzy had always wanted to eat in the cafeteria like most of the other kids did.

She replied," Oh no, I can fix our lunches in the morning from our apartment. It would be too expensive."

Tillie then understood, yet again, and calmly in a no-nonsense voice said, "I have decided that you will have fun eating at the cafeteria. Don't worry about the expense. I will see to it. Since it is Sunday today you will just go to school tomorrow and then stay through next Sunday. Now we will go for that pizza. Think about what you like. My favorite is meat lovers! We will have that and whatever you want for the second. You will have your first ride in my car. I have a red convertible so, top up or down?"

The answer was a resounding "Down!" Tillie smiled. The adventure was on.

The joyful trio almost skipped to the covered parking area. Some people used these covered garage areas for storage and some actually used them to park special cars. As it turned out, Tillie had two and used them for both functions.

The threesome climbed into the bright red Sebring. When Matteo heard the type of car it was, he chuckled, "Sebring with wings. Sebring and wing, get it?" They pretended they didn't until he explained it with great pride. Tillie invited the two to sing with her. People smiled as the oh so red car and its happy inhabitants seemed to float by. Izzy had never felt the wind in her hair before and seemed to luxuriate in it. Her head was tipped back to facilitate maximum feeling and her bright eyes were closed.

Dark came early in Florida now and the ride home would take them by houses already showing either Thanksgiving or Christmas displays resplendent with lights. One house had both and made all three giggle with the abandonment of regulations felt by the inhabitants. The turkey had a Santa head proudly displayed on its head.

When it was time for bed, Matteo sweetly pleaded that Tillie tuck him In and read a story. He asked for a Grinch story. Tillie had it. He fell asleep before the end. Izzy watched from the door as Tillie gently brought the covers up to his chin. His little face displayed a contented smile. He felt safe and relaxed as he had not for a long time.

Tillie then asked if Izzy would like to read in bed or also be tucked in. "You still are a little girl even if you have taken on adult responsibilities." Izzy looked closely at Tillie and stiffened. Someone may know too much.

Then, the little girl in her came out and she dropped her chin as she softly requested the tuck in procedure she so loved and missed. Izzy slipped into the bed that smelled of lavender. Tillie picked a book of poetry. It had been her childhood favorite and appeared to be the same for this child, as well. Izzy wanted this day to never end. But it must.

This was Izzy's week of freedom and peace, and she felt the release from worry and planning. As her tenseness released, she slipped into a dreamless sleep.

CHAPTER 34

ONDAY CAME AND IZZY AWOKE TO THE SMELL OF A REAL breakfast. She moved and the lavender smell of the sheets was so calming. Something else on her bed moved. She lay very still and felt some silk touch her leg and move up it to her shoulder. She wasn't afraid but she was curious. A snowy white silken head popped out from under the comforter. This was followed by the fast-moving body that the head belonged to and the entire cat leaped out to check out those smells. Jazzi! Where was Classi?

Izzy heard the plop of brotherly feet and the racing of fur and flesh to the site of those wonderful smells. She hesitantly slid out of bed to face a full mirror on the back of this bedroom door. Oh my! The sight was one she had to repair with some quick movement of the hairbrush she identified as her own. Tillie must have collected them last night while the children slept. Tillie knew what a girl needed for sure!

The breakfast was manna from heaven. There was no syrup for pancakes but there was honey. This was new and delicious. The discussion went to the layout of the day. Lunch would be in the cafeteria and supplied by the cafeteria. Izzy was speechless. How had this been done without effort?

The children were to finish breakfast and go to their rooms to get dressed for school. Then they were to come to walk with Tillie to the school. Izzy protested that she could walk with Matteo, but then was silenced as Tillie explained that she didn't know how to reach the school by walking and needed guidance. This was acceptable to Izzy and even seemed to please her. Did this mean that Tillie would be more involved in the day-to-day tasks in the school? She wanted to know how to go back and forth. What, exactly, did this mean?

She needed to talk to Elisha and Fjona. Did they know more about what this meant? It pleased Izzy and scared her. Malo hadn't liked this little family but Tillie definitely seemed to like them very much. How did this make sense? Matteo would not understand. If he were involved in the path her thoughts were taking her, he would say it was because of his charm. Could this be true? Izzy thought of herself as nice, but maybe not charming. "Maybe," thought Izzy, "I think too much. Maybe it is time to take a week of freedom. I will go to see the pharmacists next week."

As Matteo and Izzy walked back to Tillie's apartment, they saw the flash of furry bodies racing away down the stairs. "Ah," thought Izzie, they will be back when they are hungry or need a litter box. It seems Tillie and we are the headquarters for these two." Then she wondered if they ever took the elevator and laughed. Matteo looked at her like she was crazy.

The door was open to Tillie's apartment, and something smelled so very good. A new problem arrived in that sweet one's little head. How could they contribute to the money going into this food? She will ask Tillie this evening. For now, she noticed the two frosty glasses of milk next to home baked cookies. Izzy never wanted this to stop.

CHAPTER 35

DINNER WAS MEATLOAF WITH REAL BAKED POTATOES AND even Matteo loved the cheese topped broccoli. Tillie told him they were little trees and would make him as strong as an oak tree. After dinner they saw him trying out his muscles and seemed convinced that those biceps were bigger. The ladies looked at each other and giggled behind their hands so they would not upset his declaration.

He loved that Tillie sat down with him to watch him display his great knowledge through his homework. Their heads were over the worksheets and turned to each other to discuss his answers. He decided that he would ask his teacher for more homework, especially on new words. Tillie let him play grown up games like solitaire on her tablet after dinner and homework.

When Tillie turned to Izzy to see if she needed help, Izzy asked if they could talk. Tillie didn't know if she should be concerned or if she should laugh. She decided on neither. When Izzy was told that would be fine, she smiled with a relieved look in those beautiful photogenic eyes of hers. Izzy began with, "Matteo almost always refuses to eat vegetables. Tonight, he inhaled them and had two helpings."

Tillie agreed with a warm smile evident. "Yes, Izzy. That is called a compliment to the cook. I noticed that you ate next to nothing. Didn't you like it?" Izzy raised her eyes to Tillie, "No. It was delicious but

Matteo ate my share. I can't eat so much unless you let me help to pay for some groceries."

"Oh sweet girl, I have more than enough money to feed you. You have entertained me with your gracious acceptance. How about, if I run out of money, I will tell you? Trust me, that will not happen. I enjoy cooking for you and even I eat healthier then. You are helping in that way. I want you to be healthy so now I am, too! Do you see how that helps me?

Now, come with me and we will make you a meatloaf sandwich. This is not a request. I want you to pick out the cheese you will like melted on yours. I will have one with you and I will pick gouda. Want to experience this? It will be a science experiment, and I will tell you all about gouda or whatever you choose. OK?" Izzy was in deep thought and then nodded. She liked to be helpful.

Izzy studied Tillie carefully and thought, "How could this be the same lady we met when we first moved in? Had all this kindness and thoughtfulness always been in her and their loud joy made her sadder because they were moving into her friends' apartment?"

The sandwiches were heated in a fry pan and she learned about cheese. Who would have thought there were so many different kinds? Making and eating food was so full of taste and knowledge. They had ice cream after their sandwiches. Matteo thought he had gone to heaven.

CHAPTER *36*

I T WAS TUESDAY. THE WEEK SEEMED TO BE FLYING BY. THIS TIME THEY were allowed to walk home alone. The path seemed safe to Tillie, and she had some research to do. She was meeting with Fjona, Elisha and Mark. It was time to get everything straightened out. Just where were these parents and who was supposed to be taking care of these children? Was there anyone actually doing anything for them? Had they success-fully been caring for themselves? All of this would be exposed if Izzy won the contest and had to have a guardian step forward. They had to get ahead of it now.

In any case, they could not let these children continue on their own if there was no one named Garcia involved. If there was a couple named Garcia, they would need to represent themselves and show how they had been caring for these two little ones.

The oldest was only nine and the youngest barely six. Then, there was the liability of their parents. Were they allowing their children to be alone? After all, they had paid rent ahead for six months. Did they know that their children were alone on their own? Would this mean the parents could lose custody? Is this a crime which could keep them out of the USA?

They had to fix this before the whole thing fell apart. The parents could lose custody if the worst that could happen did just that. Tillie didn't believe that to be the case but these holes in the garment of the children's life had to be mended.

Meanwhile back at the school, Izzy was called to the principal's office. She had never done anything wrong other than sort of lying about their lives. Could the principal figure that out?

As she walked to the office, she looked down the school yard to the building Matteo was in. Should she just run in, grab him and then take off? They wouldn't be able to go back to the apartment because someone would go there to look for them. Where would they go?

What could she have done that made her have to go to the principal's office? It was the thing that every kid feared. Maybe it wasn't so bad. If it was bad, do principals have hand cuffs? Why oh why just when things had started to get better. She could always run when she found out what she had done. Maybe it wasn't too bad. OK. Decisions made. She would go to the office. Then she would run. Her teacher wasn't expecting her back so soon. She would have more time to get away.

She walked into the office and Angela looked up with a big smile on her face. Thoughts of begging Angela to tell her what this was all about ran through Izzy's mind. Then she chickened out. That would look bad. Angela looked carefully at this child who seemed to be on the edge of flight. "Oh Izzy! It is ok. It is a good thing. Don't worry. They are waiting for you in the principal's office."

"They???" That means there is more than one of "them" in the office waiting for her. Why would there be more than the principal? The assistant principal had her own office so... Angela stood and came around the counter. She took Izzy's hand and walked her into the office. She had to end this girl's panic and get things on the road.

The principal stood and another man did, too. They were both beaming. She recognized the man from the contest. He was from the Kiwanis Club. He held out his hand. Izzy looked at it and then at the principal. The principal said, "Mr. Adams is from the Kiwanis Club. He wants to shake your hand. He has something to tell you."

Just then someone stepped out from by the door with a camera. Mr. Adams said to her, "Isabella, you have won the contest for your school. The movie we took of you at the contest was judged against all the other winners over all of the entries in the county and you won for Pinellas County! Congratulations Izzy!"

The principal, Mr. Banfield then told Izzy the very thing that would scare her again, "Right after Christmas we will have a city-wide celebration for you. You have won a scholarship for when you graduate from high school. We will need your parents to come and accept the award with you. It will be on tv. We are so proud of you."

Izzy knew she was supposed to be so proud. "We will need to have your parents to sign that we can show your presentation on tv. You will be a star. Your parents and everyone who knows you will be so proud! Now I would like to take a picture with you and your principal to be hung in the office."

Izzy's mind was whirling. She just wanted to get home. Maybe she would talk to Tillie. Then she realized that she couldn't tell anyone. Everything was mind boggling for her and she didn't know what to do and where to turn. She was only nine.

CHAPTER *37*

E VERYTHING TILLIE, MARK, FJONA AND ELISHA KNEW WAS LAID
on the table. The knowledge often contradicted with known and
assumed information. Mark was aligned with the key players but knew
nothing of the Garcias. He had to talk to the Martinez parents but wasn't
due until the end of the week for a conference call. He would take the
information and lay it all out with these parents who seemed unaware.
If they had knowledge to add, such as a means to reach the Garcias, it
would alter much. This was the hope of all in the meeting. They planned
another meeting for the following Monday.

In the meantime, Tillie wasn't waiting. She had plans of her own and
would work on plans and possibilities for disclosure at the next meeting.
Action was needed and she was just the gal to kick some off.

Her brother-in-law was a private investigator. She hadn't talked to
him since the loss of her husband because he looked and sounded so
much like his brother, Tillie's late husband. It was time for her to buck
up and make that call for the safety of these children of whom she had
become so fond. She also needed to get in connection with her old
working companions.

The kiddoes should be on their way. She had to get home and have
their milk and cookies ready. Hang in there little ones. Help may very
well be on the way.

She hurried out on the immediate needs. There was her favorite bakery on the way home. Milk and cookies should be ready for those little fighters.

She got home just in time. Cookies and milk in frosted glasses were ready. Izzy had a look of determination on her face. She came in and handed a sealed envelope to Tillie. She never took her eyes off Tillie. Tillie looked at the envelope and the name on that vital piece of information. It was labeled To the Parents of Isabella Maria Martinez and marked important. Izzy had asked to be able to deliver it by hand rather than have it sent.

Tillie looked at Izzy with a quizzical expression. Izzy laid her books down and went to Tillie. She took the envelope back and tore it open. Then she handed the document inside to Tillie. The page said, CONGRATULATIONS! ISABELLA MARIA MARTINEZ is the winner of the speech writing contest. She will be representing Pinellas County through her recorded message. She has also won a Bright Futures Scholarship.

Izzy started to cry. Never should this news bring tears other than tears of joy. These were not tears of joy. Tillie went to her and held her. She was definitely going to follow through on her present plans. These will be revealed at the special meeting on Monday. Tomorrow would involve a lot of fast decisions for Tillie. She had a busy schedule after the kiddoes left for school.

For now, she held Izzy close and whispered, "Don't worry little one. You are safe. Together we can do this". Tillie thought, "What have I done? What am I about to do?" Then she hugged Izzy tighter. Izzy hugged her and wouldn't let go. Tillie sank to the floor and pulled the child onto her lap.

Izzy whispered, "What have I done? My parents…my parents…" Tomorrow, tomorrow she will worry tomorrow. It is only a day away.

Tillie raised the face of Izzy with a finger under the little chin. "Do you trust me? I am working on this. After Matteo goes to bed, we big girls will discuss this. You will be safe. You have many people on your side."

Dinner was chosen by Izzy. It was important to make her evening as peaceful as possible. Tillie told Matteo about the great thing Izzy had done. He looked at these two and asked, "So, why is she crying? Is she afraid of the big thing? Will she have to be on stage again? Maybe I can do it for her if she doesn't want to be the star. I like being on the stage. I want to be a star."

Tillie laughed and Izzy smiled. Little man had done it again. He had broken the drama and trauma without even knowing he had done so. Izzy looked at him. If what she did allowed discovery of their present life, she would be sure to let him be caught and go into one of those homes. He would be safe there with a new family. She had to find some way to be here, in place, when her parents returned. These were the plans of a nine, almost ten year old.

Would the parents get into trouble for not having a safe place for these kids? Did they not know that the Garcias had just vanished. If so, then, the government people wouldn't punish them by taking them away like the girl in her class. Her parents hadn't taken care of her so she was taken from them. She told Izzy that it was better for her. She had food and a place to be, a home where she knew what to expect. She had new parents and they loved her. She wanted that for Matteo.

She decided to not worry because Matteo would be ok no matter what happened. She wouldn't know how to get him back. She had to explain this to her parents. She wasn't living up to the agreement. But she was only nine, not even double digits.

The Garcias had failed them. She was only nine, just nine. She was tired and scared. This award should make her parents proud, but it may be the very reason why she failed the family. No one would have looked at them if she hadn't been on tv and gotten the award and scholarship. Now people were looking at her. Maybe, soon, they would be looking for them.

CHAPTER 38

T HE REST OF THE WEEK WENT ON WITH NO MORE BUMPS IN THE
road. Maybe everyone was too busy to worry about two kids who
didn't ask for any help. Maybe everyone thought the Garcias cared for
them. Maybe they would forget about the award. Maybe she could tell
the teacher and principal that she didn't want the scholarship. She didn't
need to go to college. She just wanted her life back. She wanted her parents. Matteo missed his parents, and he also missed his sister as she had
been. Monday came and the kids moved back to their apartment. The
Garcias were, supposedly, back in the picture.

Nothing had changed but the group meeting with Tillie, Mark,
Fjona and Elisha began. They had talked to Carlos and Maria and
caught them up on what was happening. The parents were very excited
about the award and immensely pleased with the college possibilities for
Izzy. Then, they were concerned because they had not been contacted
by the Garcias and were not able to contact them. They had given Izzy
a phone and put all the numbers she would need in it. They had tried to
call her but assumed that all was well. They wanted it to be fine because
they could do little about it. Worst case scenario would have been foster
homes. Now they didn't seem so bad, maybe.

The absence of the Garcia couple was a concern. No one had seen
the Garcia couple. Inquiry with the school verified this. The school had
been told by Maria that the Garcias would have the children in their

care. They never showed up at the school for any reason. This was the case when the special contest had been held. Izzy had her cheering squad, so it was overlooked

Tillie suspected that the children were alone in the apartment when they should have been in the Garcia's home. It was decided that Tillie would go to Sam's to talk to Alicia Garcia. Mark decided that they would have more success if he went along. An attorney always gets more attention and success with communication.

Tillie went to Mark's office and he drove them both to Sam's. They entered the store and asked for Alicia. He was told that she no longer worked there. The employee referred them to the office and the manager in charge. The reason for the appearance of Mark and Tillie was explained to the manager. He looked surprised. Alicia and Carlos had been picked up and he was told that they were not legally in the States. He assumed that their spouses went with them. Carlos had just been given a promotion.

An employee named Alfred had been overlooked due to the difference in his and Carlos' work ethic. The office suspected that the employee, Alfred, had been responsible. He did not get the promotion and had been overlooked again. He just wasn't floor management material. Carlos had the skills and personality for it. They had brought in management from another store and the position was being held for Carlos.

Mark and Tillie went to his office and made some phone calls. It was discovered that the Garcias had also been deported. Mark had disliked Alfred when he had taken them to the manager. He just seemed to be an evil man. His intuition had been right. Alfred had played a part in the deportation of the Garcia and the Martinez families. He asked a friend to follow through on the Garcias. They had been trying to correct their situation when snatched. It would be easier to get them reinstated so Mark handed that off. His workload was getting greater.

Sam's offered letters of intent to employ for their two lost employees to Mark to help with their reentry. They were going to be mailed to Mark. Mark would be able to use them with his quest for the Martinez.

Now the Martinez couple had a pharmacy and Sam's manager offerings of employment. The two pharmacists had gotten their manager to send a letter guaranteeing a job and sponsorship. The letters of intent were a definite plus.

Things were moving in the right direction, finally. The cruelty of the jealous coworker, Alfred, may have hastened the progress of Florida's citizenship for the Martinez couple. He wouldn't have cared. His jealousy had been realized for him when the two couples had been sent back to Mexico. This act had also served as his end for advancement. The advancement would be for the very people he had chosen to remove from his worksite. The management did not appreciate his act of vengeance.

CHAPTER 39

IZZY GOT PERMISSION TO VISIT THE OFFICE AND THE BATHROOM. SHE intended to tell them that she would like to hand her award down to the runner up. She intended to tell them that they planned to move in the future, and she wouldn't be able to be able to do what was necessary as the winner.

She slipped into the office to see two men in suits coming out of the principal's office. The principal said that they could wait right there in the office and the secretary would go for the Martinez children to bring them to the office. The principal asked, "Will Izzy and Matteo be able to continue at this school?" The men answered, "We don't know. It depends upon whether their foster home is within this area and whether we can keep them together."

Izzy froze just outside the office day. IT WAS THEM! They had come for them. They wouldn't be going home. Someone had figured out that the Garcias were not taking care of them and they were alone. It wouldn't matter that Tillie was right there for them. She lived next door and didn't have permission of the state or their parents to help. She assumed they would get Matteo first as they were headed in that direction with the guidance of Angela. Angela looked so sad. She knew what was going on and that convinced Izzy that it was the end of life as they knew it now. She couldn't save Matteo. She knew he would be ok. He was so little and so alone now. But she thought he wouldn't be alone. She must stay free to find and get him. She darted for the door to her new scary freedom.

Izzy ran as fast as those legs of hers could go. She was gulping air because crying as hard as she was and gasping for air created this need. It would take them a while to get Matteo and his "stuff". Then they would go back to the office to see if Izzy had arrived and been detained. Angela would check the girls' bathroom. Then they would regroup and head for the apartment.

Izzy raced up and into the apartment. She grabbed her old backpack and filled it with some clothes and some protein bars and water. Just then the apartment door opened and Tillie walked in. "Where is Matteo? You are home early."

The tears that had stopped in her race to escape now flowed. "They came to school. They came for Matteo and me. They took Matteo but I did escape. I have to hurry. I will leave you notes so you know I am ok. I just discovered that I love you and will miss you. I will so very much miss you. I will watch the apartment and know when Mom and Dad come home. Then I will come home too."

Tillie sank into a kitchen chair. "Izzy, you cannot run away. Where will you go? You think you are grown up but you are just a little girl. Maybe I can fix this for you. Do you trust me?"

Izzy walked closer to the open door. "I do trust you but I will only get you in trouble. You can't hide me. I don't know what to call the people who are after me but you can't try to save me. I know it will not be good for you."

Then, while Tillie opened her mouth to talk, Izzy dashed for the door. Tillie rose to stop her but wasn't successful. Izzy was going to save everyone, starting with her much beloved Tillie. They would look for her at the pharmacy, too. She didn't want them to get in trouble either. She was a dangerous refugee from the law. She ran!

As she raced through the door to her new life, she saw a strange car pull up. The two men in suits got out of the car. They had Matteo with them. As they rang the doorbell to have someone let them into the apartment, Matteo turned to look around. He saw Izzy hiding behind the entrance to the next apartment. Matteo took a step back. Would he give her up? One of the men noticed Matteo backing up and gently took Matteo's hand. This one was not getting away.

Matteo kept looking with those beautiful dark eyes of his. She threw him a kiss and he nodded. It was her goodbye for now. He turned to the man and Izzy's heart stopped. Matteo pointed to the door. The buzzer sounded. What would Matteo do? Would he give her up? Did he understand that he was to wait? She loved him and would come for him. He suddenly dashed into the building and the men followed quickly to be sure they did not lose this energetic little boy. Matteo understood. He was leading them away. He trusted his sister. He would be ok with what was happening until she came for him and come for him she would!

Matteo led them to Tillie. She told them that Izzy had been there but was now gone. "I suspect she is staying with friends. I assume you will try to get her parents back as having her on the streets would not look good for the department. She is just a little girl. I have Mark Nelson's card. He is trying to get the couple back. He may be able to help you. Bringing her parents back from Mexico will help to bring her out of hiding. The Mexican government will certainly want to please the United States. It is the USA who must make this possible. I will help in any way I can."

The two officials looked at each other. Was she helping them and Izzy or threatening them? Then they remembered that she had been an official in the unattended children department. Surely, she was trying to help. She was just thinking ahead. She just didn't want a child on the streets. It has happened before and continues to happen. This child seemed to have her own cheering section. They felt the urgency and felt their own hearts melt. For now, they were going to find a local home for the little one standing beside them. Since returning to his home and seeing his neighbor he seemed to relax. He was waiting. What was he waiting for?

CHAPTER 40

IZZY TOOK HER BACKPACK AND WALKED TO A NEARBY CHURCH. THERE was also a church school there. The afterschool activities were in full swing. She found a side door open. When she entered, she saw a small kitchen immediately to her right. She went in and looked around. There was no place to hide there so she went back into the larger meeting room. She continued to the next door. It looked like storage and there was an area she could hide in until after the building was locked. She couldn't go back to her apartment or the school now. They would be looking for her. This was a perfect refuge. She had enough food and books to hide out until the weekend.

The weekend came and she continued to hide. The pastor's office was near her hiding place and he was there early and late. She thought they only worked on Sunday. Finally, it settled down enough to let her sneak to the exit. Cars were appearing and people were settling in the larger room off the kitchen. There was a hall that offered some protection from exposure. The people sat at tables and chairs and began the meeting (Bible Study). Izzy was now in the kitchen for protection from detection. She listened to the conversations and really wanted to stay but knew that she would then lose her chance to get out. They were talking about salvation and she really needed that!

Finally, she took a chance and whipped around the short hall to freedom. She felt kind of sad leaving this space. She had felt so safe there and now she was moving to a darkening world. She successfully managed to make her way to the Seminole City shopping area. She slipped from area to area and no one seemed to notice her. She hid best in the throng of happy shoppers. If someone looked too closely at her, she simply joined the closest group of shoppers.

She continued to her apartment. She stood across the street and watched the lights go on. She felt a strange kind of ache in her mind and body. Was that caused by the desire to be there, in there and behind that dark window on the third floor? She saw the light go on in what she thought was Tillie's apartment. That did it. She was going in.

She got to Tillie's door and got out paper and pencil from her backpack. She penned the following. Tillie, I really miss you. You cannot open your door or I will have to run. You cannot see me because if they ask you, I don't want you to lie and then go to jail. I know you would go to jail for me. I would go for you, too. We could talk. Can you open your door to hear me better? I just want to hear your voice. They have Matteo. Can you find out if he is ok and then we can talk again? She pushed the note under the door as she did one knock. Maybe that would be easier for Tillie to notice.

She waited and held her breath. She didn't want anyone to hear her breathe. This was a reflex for her and about the time she had to take that breath the door inched open. Izzy crouched low on the door mat. If that door opened farther, she was ready to run.

"Hi sweetheart. You had me worried. I won't ask you where you have been but I hope you were safe. Are you hungry? I have fresh soup and bread and even Haagen Daz ice-cream bars. I will leave the door open a bit and you can come in. While we talked, I put the soup in the microwave and buttered the bread. It is on my table. If you feel safer, you can leave your key on the table and I will get a copy made so I can put some goodies out for you."

Izzy immediately took off the chain around her neck and tossed it into the apartment. She added, "Could you keep me up on what is going on with Matteo and my parents?"

The response was, "Yes, I will close this door when I return from reading the book in my room. The spare room is all made up for any-one wanting to join the girls who are in there now. They sleep in there almost every night. I think they are waiting for someone. They would like the door open just a bit to allow them to come and go more easily. A mystery guest could come and eat and then go to the guest room. Then I will put the dishes in the dishwasher. I picked up your schoolbooks and assignments. Your teacher, Sarah, is doing this on the sly in case anyone would hear from you."

When Tillie came back to her kitchen the dishes had been rinsed and placed in the dishwasher. Tillie felt the weight of the moment. She was offering to give her a safe place to be and Izzy would only accept if there was no way that Tillie would be impacted. It could be handled under Izzy terms. For tonight the little one was safe. She had her plans and was busy making things work. It would take some time and until then the game would be played with those Izzy terms. Tillie did not want her to disappear again.

Why did life have to be so difficult? One could not go back and change the things that brought on this chain or misfortune. No one wanted this child to be out there on her own. She was only nine. Izzy was gone in the morning. It was as if she had never been there. Tillie suspected that she was next door, fearful and hiding.

In the morning the first thing on her agenda was the stop at the hardware store for another key. The next stop was the grocery store. This child wouldn't or couldn't go to either of these stops. When she got home she found the homework on her table. She went next door with the key and groceries. The door wasn't locked.

Tillie sang, "Coming in, oh coming in!" She heard the bedroom door open. Out marched the girls. She showed them their bag of treats and they plurrrrted in approval which then required five treats each! The appearance of the girls was all the evidence Tillie had needed to determine that Izzy was there.

She put the key next to the food and then left to allow Izzy to note what food was there as she put it away. She would then be aware of the food and know it belonged to her. Surely no one would look for her in the apartment because they wouldn't know that the rent was prepaid. It would be assumed that she was on the street or with an unknown person. Tillie would not be suspected in any capacity.

Tillie went home with a sigh of relief. Tomorrow, she would bring her a set of headphones so she could enjoy the television with sound. Now there was evidence of another hurricane coming. They were going to name this one Sara. There could not be a worse time for a child to be homeless and on her own. There had to be divine intervention to have placed such wonderful caring adults in the path of Izzy and Matteo. For now, she had the protection of those wonderful intuitive furry angels.

CHAPTER *41*

T ILLIE THOUGHT ABOUT THE HURRICANE THAT WAS FORMING. SHE decided that Izzy needed the headphones now so she could hear that it was not certain yet. Seeing the pictures without words would be terrifying for a little girl. She found a set of earphones and went to put it in Izzy's apartment. She opened the door slowly and stated that she was dropping off the headsets for use that evening.

The next morning, she chose a couple of her plants and put them beside the next door. She included a note stating that they should be set in the windows for sunshine. There was a plan there, a reason for the move of her African violets named Sam and Iam. In case Izzy was there she didn't want to betray that she knew it. Izzy must be free to come to her when she needed to and under Izzy terms. Right now, it was sort of like making a feral cat feel safe. True, Izzy didn't want Tillie to get into trouble but it was more than that, too.

She also had the cats to tell her when Izzy was there. They would come early and Tillie would treat and feed them. Suddenly the twosome would go to the door and stand tall to turn the knob. Classi always turned the knob and Jazzi always leaned her weight on the door to get it to swing out. What a clever pair they were.

Later in the morning Tillie got a call from Matti's foster mom, Sue. Tilli knew that Sue was at capacity with Matteo. Izzy would be a problem. Matteo wanted to come to talk to Tillie. An afternoon date was set

108

and Sue would bring Matteo to Tillie's. He needed to see her and his apartment to know everything was still ok.

The two kids were establishing their bond to life as it had been and could/should be again. It was a touching moment when the bell announced that they were there and were asking permission to enter the building. That had to have been a tough moment for Matteo. He was locked out before he could even get near to what he loved. Then there was the tap on the door.

Tillie opened the door to let the cats swoop in. Sue and Matteo stood on the mat. Tillie reached for Matteo and put her arm around his shoulders to pull him in. Matteo had different ideas. He wrapped his arms around Tillie and began to sob. Tillie felt the tears fall, too. She couldn't have stopped those tears if she had tried. At that point she vowed to follow through with the plans she had begun.

Sue looked touched and waited for Tillie to unravel the hug. It was a bit difficult as the cats had joined in and were sitting on her bent knees with front paws on the shoulders of Matteo. The cats saw the treat bag on the counter and disengaged to run, jump and knock! It was a trick they had taught these humans. It worked as Matteo ran to pick up the treats from the floor and look at Tillie to allow dispersal as the cats had taught him. Tears were replaced with smiles all around (Yeah, the cats, too).

Sue stepped back. She stated, "This little boy has been very quiet. I think that is not normal for him and that is what his teacher has confirmed. His teacher, Sarah, says that he keeps looking at the door of the classroom. She believes he is looking for his sister. I think he feels lost himself and is worried that his sister is in trouble. Right now, I think it is his chance to talk about some of these worries. Everyone is worried about his sister. I am the most worried about him. I hope he isn't thinking about running away to find his sister.

I was going to stay and join in the conversation, but I think it would be better for me to go shopping. I will come back to get him when you call. My friend is watching the rest of the gang. It is tablet time now!"

With that last statement Sue steps in to hug her friend and give

Matteo her big smile. "He is not ready to hug me yet but when he is, I will be so happy. I want to help him if he lets me."

Matteo makes eye contact with Sue and then steps toward her. She kneels to let him talk if he just will! He reaches out and hugs her. The hug is returned. Then he gives her a faint smile and turns to Tillie. Sue turns quickly to leave with tears hidden but Tillie knows and gently shuts the door. Matteo is in a good place. Now is the time to start to mend his heart, maybe even help his mind.

CHAPTER 42

MATTEO LOOKS UP WITH AN ARM AROUND EACH CAT. CLASSI WAS licking his tears away and Jazzi dashed off to bring him a white furry mouse. Healing had begun. Now it was Tillie's turn. It was a beginning with only one way for it to be complete. The girls ran to the couch and curled up at the end as if to listen. They definitely were telling Tillie to begin.

Tillie started it, "Well, you have my good friend Sue very worried. Are you planning to try to run away?"

"I am thinking about it. I could find Izzy. She must think I left her. I need her. She is my sister." A tear rolled down his cheek.

"I have news for you. Izzy missed you, too. I am trying to do something to bring you back together but you must help. I know you can't turn off how you feel. You are lonely, scared and helpless. That is how it will be as you are loved and some of those people are not here. The people who are here want to help you. They are worried that you will make some bad choices and make things worse for your sister. She knows you are ok and she only must take care of herself now. She is only nine. Do you understand?"

Matteo bit his lower lip and swallowed hard. "Yes, I think so. You think I am going to run away. Maybe I am. I have to wait for the right time because my legs are not so long. That is the bad choice, right?"

Tillie got up and walked to the kitchen. Matteo watched with big eyes and what she had said to him began to make sense. She came back with some chips and a glass of soda for each of them.

Matteo slid to the floor. "Crumbs," he said. She smiled and instead of telling him it was ok, she slid to the floor beside him. He added, "Ok, I won't run away. I will try to smile and quit watching for Izzy. I have you, right?" He looked into her eyes with an intensity unusual for such a small child. He wanted only one answer from her.

"Absolutely! We have each other and we will work together to get Izzy back. I know you know that Sue is at capacity for children so I will work on finding someplace where you can be together. Will that make you happier? We are also working hard at getting your parents back. They are not lost but have things to do before they can come back. It is hard for you to understand so you just must understand that Mark, Fjona, Elisha and I are working on it. Do you believe that? So, your sister is not lost and your parents are not lost. They all have things to do before they can come back. You are safe and they need to know that you will be good and not run away. It is one thing less to worry about. What do you think?"

Matteo had not moved during her talk, and she had watched him closely as she talked. She saw that he was also watching her with an intense desire to input. She could see that he was understanding, but would he agree? Would he be truthful? Would she know his true feelings and intent? She had only known him to tell the truth, but he was stressed and felt alone with adult sized worries.

Matteo looked down at his treat and picked up the glass. He was thirsty. "When you cried did you lose moisture? Probably," was his thought as his throat seemed to be stuck shut. He took a drink and looked seriously at Tillie. "OK. I don't want to make you worry. All the kids at school have grandmas and grandpas. Izzy and I don't. I want to adopt you. How can I do that?" Tillie knew better than to laugh. This was a serious moment. He had, evidently, been thinking about it. Here was a family member he could touch. He needed that.

Her reply was delivered with the serious tone it required. "Well, I think you just did. I accept. We must drink a toast to make it official."

She raised her glass of soda. He lifted his and she gently tapped them together. The deed was done.

That is what Tillie thought. Then he said, "Family people have the same name sometimes. My mom calls me Matti once in a while. You can be Matti, too as your name is really Matilda. You could be Mattigram or Tilliegram. I like Mattigram as it is like me. Gram is short for Gramma. Tillie thought very hard or pretended to do so. Then, to Matteo's delight she said, "I will be Mattigram, and I will sometimes call you Matti. They both beamed and were cheered by cat chirps! OK, now it was done, right?

Tillie had a new worry. It had been two days since she had seen or heard Izzy. She had told Izzy to keep the soil damp but not wet for Sam and Iam. The little waterer with a bit of African violet fertilizer was at the same level. They didn't need water yet but would she come in time? Tillie would water them but didn't like to take away this sign of Izzy's coming and going. Even the cats looked worried. They had come today because they seemed to know that Matteo would be appearing. Tillie did not like having her gone for even one day.

CHAPTER *43*

IZZY HAD TRIED TO GO TO THE APARTMENT. SHE HAD QUIETLY MOVED up the stairs and then stopped. She saw a lady entering Tillie's apartment. What she did not know was that the lady was picking up her brother. She heard Tillie's voice of welcome. She had never seen the lady before so was a bit worried that this person could still be looking for her. She really wanted to be found but then remembered that it was not what her parents had wanted. Once they were in the "system" as Tillie had called it, the harder it would be to get them out. Izzy backed down a step or two and then quietly ran out. She hoped the flowers would be ok.

Lights in the church were on and there were people coming and going. It was Saturday and that was when it was very busy. People were meeting in that big room again. A lady entered and went into the little kitchen. Izzy followed her in like she was with her and then continued into the main part of the church. Someone had left the door to another area open, so she went through like she had a mission, and no one stopped her. She was in school! This church had a school! There was a bathroom and a big kitchen. The classroom doors were all open, so she walked down the hall and peeked into each room. She felt safe and strangely at peace. She may be hungry, but she was safe.

She could hear that the church service was breaking up. Church people are nice, she thought and felt an irresistible desire to join them. She walked into the line to greet the minister. The group she was closest to had Gretchen and Mark. Kindness just seemed to emanate from them. There was also a Bonnie who said she had brought some donuts into the small kitchen for people who needed food to take. That was her! She needed food!

Gretchen was talking about choir practice. Oh, how she wanted to belong. She had immediately felt alone and yet safe all at the same time. She walked into the small kitchen and spied the donuts. She took a package of 6. She was pretty sure Tillie needed a donut, too. Then she slipped out and back into the area where the service had taken place. She moved into the small area adjacent and then to the slightly open door to the school. She was set for the night.

Morning came and she heard the school coming to life. Since she had slept in the kitchen, no one saw her. Again, the feeling of being alone came like a lightning strike. She was amazed to find that not only did she miss Matteo and her parents, but she also missed Tillie. When they were back as a family would Tillie shut her door to them like before? She swallowed hard to stop the tears. Why did life have to be so hard? She had appreciated her life before but now…she ached for it back.

She slipped out of the school the next morning with her backpack minus four of the donuts which had been donated for last night's dinner and this morning's breakfast. As she exited the church she saw a place for donations. There was nothing in it until she slipped one of her dwindling dollars into it.

She left but looked back. This church on the corner had been a salvation for her. What do other lost children do if they don't have a church? Did people really sleep on the streets like the man on the tv had said?

She knew that she was too young to be out on her own, so she often joined groups of adults and acted like she belonged. If they noticed her, she simply changed groups and they just thought she was with whatever group she joined.

She mused that her classmates had talked about kids who slept in alleys who were homeless. She thought this was in other countries, but she did not know for sure. She had not paid that much attention. She didn't see any alleys soooo.

As she walked through the stores, she heard a group talking about the tropical storm named Rafael being gone. Wait! Now they were talking about a new storm that was going to be named Sara. They shouldn't name it that! Storms were bad and scary. Her teacher named Sara was none of those things. She really admired Sara. She feared storms.

Suddenly she needed Tillie. With that thought she sidled out of the stores. She needed to wash her clothes and take a bath before she saw Tillie. It was Saturday and people were home in the other apartments. What should she do? She would ask Tillie, but she didn't want her to see her before a clean-up, but it was Saturday. Tillie was always so clean which she called tidy. Izzy loved the way Tillie talked.

As she walked, she saw a police car. It pulled over to her and called, "Hey! little girl!" She hurried to catch up to the lady with three kids and asked one of them, "Do you go to school at that church over there? You look familiar?" The little girl turned to talk to Izzy and the police car drove away. They would, however, report a possible sighting.

CHAPTER 44

I ZZY DECIDED TO CHANCE IT AND STARTED THE WALK TO HER APART- ment, a walk to Tillie. As she walked, she heard the sounds made by a slow-moving police car. She turned and saw a police car headed in her direction. She started to run and tripped. Her shorts and tops were torn and her shoes scuffed. She had scrapes on her knees. She got up and started to run. The car was getting closer and then it moved on past her and pulled over a car. It had not been after her. She kept running. She looked damaged, and she didn't want the police to turn their attention to her.

When she stopped to catch her breath and realized that she had lost her backpack and those precious donuts she had saved for Tillie. For a reason known only to her, this was the final straw. She stopped sobbing and looked at her hands and assumed the same was true of her face. She was an absolute dirty mess. She didn't know where she was. She remem- bered reading this book about a family that had gotten lost and retraced their steps. She looked back at the way she had come. There were no steps to follow. She just saw blocks of concrete sidewalks. She started to trudge back the way she had come.

Tillie just couldn't go on without knowing where the child had vanished. There were so many things that could happen to a little one on her own. She looped out block by block from the apartment building. She prayed as she drove.

Three blocks from her origination site and she saw a pitiful limping and bowed over individual. She couldn't stop as she wanted to help this person but was on a mission. She came to a dead end and had to turn around. She had called in help for the poor creature she had passed. Now she looked at the person again and decided that she had to pull over and give her immediate help. She could take her to a site for medical help and then make sure she got to a place where she could rest and recover. She got out of her car and called, "Excuse me, I would like to help you. I will not hurt you!"

Izzy heard the voice of an angel and fell to the sidewalk exhausted and bleeding. She started to weep and reach her arms toward Tillie. Tille gasped and ran to scoop up the little girl. They both collapsed on the sidewalk. Both were crying. Izzy stopped crying and used her dirty little hands to wipe away the Tillie's tears. This left Tillie looking like a raccoon. Izzy insisted on walking back to the car with the help of her personal angel.

As they drove back, they noticed Izzy's backpack. It was right where they turned to head home. Tillie went out of the car to get it. It looked fine. Izzy had not fallen on it. Izzy looked as delighted as possible after what she had just gone through.

Izzy collapsed on the seat of the convertible as it hurried to get them home. She said, "When I get there I will lie down on the floor in my apartment. I don't want to get anything dirty and I can't run the water until after everyone one else is making noise. I don't want anyone to know I am there.

Entering the apartment building had Izzy heading toward the staircase. Tillie took her scraped up little hand and directed her to the elevator. Izzy moaned "no. everyone uses the elevator and they may see me."

Tillie said, "I will just tell them we have been out skateboarding." Izzy looked puzzled. Was this a joke? Tillie laughed. Then Izzy joined her. It was a joke. When they got to their apartments, Tillie pulled her into her apartment. It was too clean. Izzy pulled back. Tillie was persistent. Tillie put on the tv and told Izzy to relax as she put on the Hallmark channel. "Stay here and rest. I will be right back."

Izzy heard running water. When Tillie came back and took Izzy's hand to lead her to a fragrant bubble bath. "Soak and relax as I get you a change of clothes. This is the beginning of a change for you. No more hiding. This is enough. No more." It was said with such determination that Izzy complied with a sigh of relief but yet uncertainty. Just who was this powerful lady? She was scary but exciting…just what Izzy needed. Her part of this fight was over.

Tillie returned with pajamas and a bathrobe. They were going nowhere. They were having a sleepover. She left them in the guest bedroom where Izzy seemed to have returned while wrapped in a towel and fallen asleep.

Izzy awoke to the smell of chocolate. She came out of the bedroom with her pajamas on and the too small bathrobe. Izzy went to her backpack and proudly brought out the donuts. They were crushed and crooked. Izzy looked distressed. Tillie went to the cupboard and got out plates and silverware. Next, she went to the refrigerator and came out with spray on cream topping. They glued the donuts together with the spray. It was pretty good!

CHAPTER 45

I T WAS EARLY AFTERNOON. AFTER THE SUGARY TREAT, IZZY WAS BAN-
daged and placed in front of the tv with the remote. Tillie picked up
the phone. She had Mark's private home number, so she skipped right
to that. She was done with this pussyfooting around. Matteo was safe
but sad and in "the system" Izzy was to be the focus. She was only nine.

Mark didn't answer the call until after the third refusal to leave a
message and redial. He answered, "Tillie, are you ok?"

Tillie responded, "I have Izzy. I found her on the sidewalk with her
clothes torn and scrapes all over her. I don't care what happens to me
for harboring her. This is what we will do. I will try my best to hasten
the process for me to be their foster home. That would be the fastest
but I want you to get ahold of the Martinez parents. They are to assign
custody of these two and I will accept that assignment. Do both at the
same time. Get your resources to help me be qualified and assigned
these children. That will free up Sue for a child. She cannot have them
both and they need to be together. Do what you must as best you can.
I know you. Starting now, Izzy is with me. If you want to keep it quiet
so that you do not cause a legal problem and interference with my foster
request, so be it. BUT, hurry."

There was silence followed by this promise by Mark. "I will push
every legal favor owed to me. I have many favors due me. On that, I
promise!" The phones were hung up starting with Tillie. This was the

Tillie who used to exist before pain and loss took her down. She was on fire! Mark was dialing.

Izzy looked up at her angel, her guardian. Tillie smiled sweetly. Gone was the terror that had taken Mark to task and started the beginning of the end. Tillie's soft voice said, "We need to move your essential things over to here. We will use your apartment at times, but life will continue for you from here. There should be no more hiding soon. I am not taking your power to be you away from you but I am giving you a break from all that stress. Now, how about a special dinner. I can make it or we can order in."

Izzy looked up and said, "You decide." Both broke into peals of laughter. "I think we will call and ask Elisha and Fjona to join us." Added Tillie.

Within an hour the door got a little tap. The special guests had sneaked in when tenants left before the door closed completely. The hall was full of the smell of pizza with no onions but tons of meat. Fiona rushed in and oohed over the bandages while Elisha announced her own good news. They were excited about this news and eager to share.

What a day! Tragedy turned Joyful. The pharmacy had been able to find a pharmacist who only wanted six months or less to fill in until Maria could be back. Even the hurricane to be, Sara, joined in the celebration as she was downgraded on the tv forecast. More would be known mid-week. So very much more!! The neighbors must have thought that the quiet Matilda was having a party!

Over pizza, Tillie explained what had happened and that she had decided to back up the progress of this quest with all the power she had left from her former working days. She knew people and Monday would be very busy. Fjona and Elisha promised to call Mark and see how they could help. They were sponsors for the Martinez couple. They could check on the progress to get Maria certified as a pharmacist in the states.

Focus first and foremost, the children would be brought home and united under the guardianship of Matilda Lee Green. When told this Izzy added. "Yes, we have two homes. One is now empty and the other is this one so filled with love." This was meant to be. Mattigram was going to achieve this at any cost.

CHAPTER 46

Sunday morning came. Tillie opened her eyes to look directly into the sparkling eyes of a mummy child. Fjona and Elisha had wrapped all wounds no matter how small, with gauze. Izzy's long dark red hair framed a face that should be painted as the face of an angel. Izzy started to laugh and those dark eyes simply sparkled. A glance to the right found greenish gold eyes in one face and bright blue in the other face. Tillie began to laugh. What joy these three had brought to her life. She had never seen Izzy so relaxed and happy. The cats were purring.

"Well, well" said Tillie. "What a lineup of beauties!"

Izzy crooned, "You should be in this lineup then!"

The cats demanded that they were to celebrate as well and did not want coffee with cream or not. Freeze dried treats were brought out for them.

"What would you like to do today?" asked the heroine of this group.

"Do you think…is it possible…. maybe, to see Matteo? "asked Izzy.

Tillie replied, "Mark thinks we are taking a chance by having you live here all the time. I don't want to do anything if there is even a possibility of messing things up. Do you think Matteo can be quiet about it?"

Izzy laughed. "I don't think he has changed. I have you and he has Sue. We can wait. I have now decided that you will fix this. You are my heroine. I looked that up on Google. A boy is a hero."

"Well, let us figure out what we are going to do. How would you like this day to go now that we agree? Let us start with a cup of coffee!"

"I get coffee! Really!!? What a grown-up thing!"

Izzy's coffee was dressed up so it was mostly cream. She was thrilled with her crème-colored coffee. The discussion moved to a decision to go to a park for a picnic. They would go far enough away that no one would know them. It was a break to not hide, run or worry.

Most of the work was now in the hands of Mark. They would give him the week and then call him on Friday. Although they all wanted the Martinez couple back with their children, the focus and immediate need was to have these children in safe locations.

Mark had reported to them that the Garcias had intended to help with the care of the children but were deported on the same day as the Martinez couple. What a mess this had caused!

The money to pay weekly for this care was still under Izzy's bed. She had not spent much of it. The apartment had been well stocked.

Izzy looked at Tillie and then asked. "Could we bring our tree over here? We need to have a Christmas tree here. Our tree just appeared. Matteo thinks the girls brought the tree for us. They come and go like they have special powers. Maybe when I am ten, I will know about these things." Izzy looked at Tillie for the answer.

"Well," answered Tillie, "Adults do not know everything. It is true that you learn every year but many things we do not understand. I know a lot about some things. Other adults know a lot about other things. If it interests you, then you learn more about it. You will learn a lot about what you want to do when you grow up. Your Mom is a pharmacist. She knows a lot about that. What do you want to be when you grow up?"

Izzy looked like she was looking far away. Then she said, "I had wanted to work in a hospital with little kids. Now I want to do something for little kids who are lost in the streets. What would that be?"

Tillie responded, "Well, you can still do that while working at a hospital. We will investigate that. I think when you are older you will know for sure."

Izzy sweetly responded, "When I am ten?"

Tillie smiled as she responded, "Perhaps we will talk about this again when you are ten. For now, I think we should go for a ride with the top down. We would find a great park and have our picnic there. Let us pack special food and put on crazy bright clothes.

So, they did. Izzy wore a scarf over her hair to hide the red hair and also to keep the hair from wildly blowing into her face. Tillie wore a hat. The adventure was on!

CHAPTER *47*

MATTEO SAT STILL WITH HIS LITTLE HANDS FOLDED TOGETHER. This was not the little boy Sue had been told about. The rest of her gang were excited about their special pizza and dessert to celebrate Matteo becoming a part of their group.

Sue sat down by him and asked, "You have new friends here and the love of this charming group of children and me. Do you feel like talking?"

Matteo looked up, "No, not really. What do you want to talk about?"

"Each one of these children has a story. Some are sweet but promising and some scary but about to change. They didn't talk at first either. They felt different than other children. They felt hurt. Do you have a story? We can start with me being your audience."

Matteo looked up, "Why?" he asked.

"Well," Sue said, that is a start. "I was hoping for a bit more. Do you want to know why and how you ended up here?"

"I know why I am here. I don't have parents here in our country. I know how I got here. Somebody grabbed me. I like you and the kids but I miss my sister, my parents and my Mattigram. I know they love me. I know Izzy lives everywhere and can't take me but I want my Mattigram and she could have me. Why can't I go to her again?"

Sue felt his pain and replied, "I think it would be ok for me to take you to visit her. We are trying to make it ok for you and your sister to go to her to live until your parents come. I don't know if we can or when we can, but we will try. In the meantime, can you try to be ok here? Everyone is sad for you and they need to feel happy. They really do. You must trust me about that. Can you help me to make my other kids happy?"

Matteo raised his head and looked at the other kids. He thought they looked ok. While he looked at them, he saw little Rebecca look up at him with sad eyes. She was the youngest at just 4. He turned to Sue and said, "Ok. I will play with Rebecca even though she is just a little kid. I don't want her to feel lonely like I do. But I want to go alone to see my Mattigram. Can we make that deal?"

Matteo's answer was a hug and an arm around his shoulders and then, Sue added, "Sure. We were just donated a tablet. Would you show her how to use it?"

The next time Sue gazed at her tribe she saw Matteo sitting on the couch with Rebecca as close as she could be. He was showing her how to use the tablet. He looked so proud when she was able to successfully take her turn at the simple puzzle they were working on. He looked up and saw her watching. He gave her a wink and a thumbs up. He was the big kid, the leader now.

"Great job, you two." murmured Sue, as she joined the little twosome.

Matteo answered, "I think I can teach her lots. She seems pretty smart. Now, about my Mattigram..." Deal made. Maybe they can make it even more special.

CHAPTER 48

THE TREE HADN'T MOVED FROM THE MARTINEZ APARTMENT. IZZY had acknowledged that the night before. She had hoped to have it in Tillie's apartment. It might mean that Christmas would be celebrated with Tillie in her home. She went to bed with hopes still in place.

When Izzy woke up, she heard noises. Tillie had guests. People were laughing and talking. It frightened Izzy. They had found her and now Tillie would be in trouble for harboring her. It was a new word she had heard when she had listened to a phone conversation between Tillie and Mark. The were coming to get her into that unknown "system" and take Tillie someplace even more scary. But they wouldn't be laughing. The clincher to that thought was the sound of Tillie laughing. So, then what? Who were these happy invaders?

She peeked out her door but didn't want to come out and risk losing her new home with Tillie. She desperately wanted to join these happy laughing people. Tillie walked them to the door and handed them money. Izzy saw this through the slit in the door. They had delivered something. The smell gave her a clue. She still held her ground and didn't move.

"Cinnamon, butter and coffee" she whispered as if voicing them would make them more real then they already were! Izzy couldn't stand waiting but feared discovery.

The soft sounds of Christmas music could be heard. It was in her bedroom with her. This must be the sound system Tillie had told her about and Matteo had all but drooled over. Then Tillie was singing. She had a beautiful soft soprano voice. Finally, she heard the words she was waiting for with such great desire. "Izzy, would you like to have breakfast and then help me?" Tillie came into her room. Izzy felt arms around her as a gentle voice said, "Yes, sweet Isabella. This is for you and I and Matteo soon, too."

A tall evergreen stood in front of the windows. A star touched the ceiling aglow with magic. The tree shown with silver and gold lights. Since it was early it was just dark enough to display the tree in its true beauty. For this little girl it was beyond beautiful. It was magical and full of the hope of Christmas. Izzy was speechless in awe. She turned into those arms and cried softly into the shoulder of the woman who had made this happen for her.

She gently pushed back from Tillie and said, "Do I smell cinnamon rolls? Were those really tall elves that were here? I so love you. Matteo wants to make you our grandmother and rename you Mattigram. I like Tilliegram better. What do you think? We don't have grandmothers and if we did none could be better than you. You get to choose. You can say no."

"Hmmmm. I thought I was your grandmother. Oh wait, not at first! Well then, the answer is yes to the grandma designation and a yes to different names for both of you to call me. How wonderful! Let us celebrate with warm cinnamon rolls and beverage of choice."

CHAPTER *49*

MATTE WAS SAFELY IN SCHOOL AND IZZY WAS STILL SLEEPING. Did she not want to deal with reality and life as it is now? Tillie was in deep thought. When Izzy woke up Tillie had to ask her to do something that would terrify her.

She wanted Mark to get their parents back by Christmas but until then there was a possibility of change for them that would frighten and then please them. Mark and she were doing all that was possible. She hoped to have an intermediate change in their lives that would bring some joy.

Everything was so difficult. The parents were doing all they could to be good citizens one day. The unforgiveable part was not keeping track of the responsibilities necessary to become responsible citizens. They had done all they could for the children but these little citizens were suffering their loss. The need to give them hope was a given but letting them hope too much and then not delivering would be cruel. Promises had to be realistic.

Then the phone rang. Tillie heard the news she had been waiting for. Her major part in this could now be a possibility. She would have to leave Izzy for a while but it was necessary. Things were going in the right direction, finally.

The next call was not the one she expected. Fjona was on the phone. Sue had called Fjona to report that Matteo was missing. He had run from the school. He had told his friend, Richie, that he was going to find his sister.

The Social Services that handled foster care had put out an Amber alert on him. This elevated his status in the "system". Only specially trained foster care could handle these children. Sue was so trained but stated that she would take him back. However, she was at maximum capacity with Matteo. She suggested they place him in a home where they can also take the sister when she is found. The Martinez children were missing.

Tillie picked up her phone to make a call. She got the answer she wanted. When asked how she knew about these children, Tillie confirmed what she had stated earlier. She had discovered critical information found in their files. The report stated that she was a neighbor of the family when they were intact. She was now a licensed foster parent.

Matteo ran as fast as he could. He ran in the direction he thought was correct. The problem was that he had never really paid attention. Why should he? He had his big sister and that was her job. His job was to hold her hand and love life. He was very good at his job. This created a problem for him right now. Thinking ahead was not his forte. He was pretty sure he could wait until he was nine and then it would just come to him. Unfortunately, he could not wait until he was nine.

Then he remembered what his current job was. He was trying to find Izzy. Then they could go to Tillie or back to school. What if she refused? He thought Sue was very special but he wanted Tillie and Izzy. He knew that his parents were not in this country. He wasn't sure what that meant. After all, he had Izzy. The problem now was that he did not have Izzy. No one could find her but she would know he needed her and just show up. She always did.

It was getting dark and he was hungry and tired. He remembered his teacher saying that if you ever got lost find a policeman. Richie told him to go in a circle so you didn't get too far away before someone found you. That didn't make any sense as you don't run away to be found. Izzy would know he needed her. She had never failed him before. He was pretty sure that was the job of big sisters. It was the job of his big sister in any case.

He saw a Chick Filet restaurant. That made his tummy growl. He walked to one of his favorite restaurants before he realized that he had no money. He stood in line with a large family. They all ordered. He did, too. The parents stood to the side talking. When everyone had their food they paid. They didn't notice that they had paid for him, too. He took his food and went outside. The kids were all looking at him as he left but didn't report it to their parents. The parents were too busy picking up condiments.

"So," he thought, "this is how kids without sisters or parents get to eat." His big concern now was where he would sleep. He saw police cars circling the area. He was supposed to go to a policeman if he was lost, not a police car. There were so many rules and he did not know them all. Actually, he only knew those two rules about running away. Going in circles had not helped him. He would tell Izzy and Richie about the new one he had discovered about eating with no money. Finding a policeman was hard because none of these policemen walked.

He slipped along the roads to the shopping area. He went into one of the stores that had all these wonderful Christmas things. He had been to Home Goods with his mother before so he knew the floor plan. In the back farthest corner were all these things that were piled up. There was a door to a back room. Back there were no people but lots of pillows and blankets. He pushed through to the bottom of the box of pillows with a blanket. He would put it back after just a little nap.

CHAPTER 50

Matteo climbed out to find that the entire store was dark. This was not covered by his two rules of running away. All the doors were locked. Suddenly a police car arrived. Policemen got out. He ran to the door. They were out of their cars and so legal according to one of the rules. He got scared when he saw they had guns. Do they shoot little kids without big sisters? The man without a uniform unlocked the door. He scrunched down and covered his head. They couldn't see him was his thought.

A gentle hand touched him and lifted his arm making him stand. "Well, little man, how did you get in here? Are you alone?"

Matteo whispered, "No, I have a big sister but she isn't here now. I was looking for her. Can you help me find her? Am I arrested? Do you shoot kids without sisters? I don't know all the rules about running away."

The policeman smiled and put his arm around the back of this lost boy. "Never. Who are you and where is your family? Are they trying to find you? Are you Matteo? We have been looking for you. It is late but people are waiting up for you. Want to go home?"

"Matteo said, "No. No one is at my home. I need to find my sister. Can you find her so I can go back to be with Sue and her kids? Then Izzy can come there too until my parents get home."

"We will take you to be with Sue but you must promise to never run away again. You didn't run away from her so that is why you get to go back there. The school you ran from will have to be told that you have been found. After that, I am not sure what will happen but you won't go to school tomorrow."

Matteo started to sob, "I just wanted to find my sister. She always tells me what to do but she is lost. She ran away. I thought that if I ran away I would be able to find her or she would find me. I don't want my teacher or Sue to be mad at me or be in trouble. I want Izzy. Please! I want my Izzy."

The policeman said, "Right now we will call everyone. You don't need to be scared. No one will shoot you. We don't shoot little boys even when they somehow break into stores. I am Officer Hanson and I have two little boys, too. Now we will go someplace safe."

With that made clear Matteo and his new friend went out of the store and Matteo got his first ride in an official police car.

Matteo was taken back to be with Sue. She was very worried about him. She fed him peanut butter toast and milk and the adventures of run-away Matteo came to an end.

In the morning Matteo was taken to a building that was large and official looking. Maybe policemen don't shoot burglar kiddos but could they put him in jail? (Well reader, soon you and Matteo will find out.)

CHAPTER *51*

H E WAS TAKEN TO A ROOM. SUE WAS WITH HIM AND HE CLUTCHED her hand very tightly. The lady in the room asked him why he ran away. The friendly lady asked him, "Did someone at school scare or hurt you? Did anyone hurt you?"

Matteo was scared and held onto the hand of Sue. "I was looking for my sister. She ran away before."

The door opened and the principal from the school came in and repeated the same question. Matteo stared at him. He thought, "Boy, am I in big trouble now. The principal wasn't smiling."

"That was a very unsafe thing for you to do. You could have been hurt. You must tell us why you decided to do what you did." Matteo started to cry and said, "I am sorry. I wanted to find my sister. I need my Izzy. Please help me."

This little boy could not have been sadder. Then a big surprise was revealed to him. The mysterious lady said, "You must make a promise to me and we will find your sister. If you run away again, we will not trust you and cannot promise you that you will be with your sister again. Do you understand that? You will both be safe but not together. Do you know why?"

"Yes. You think that if we both run away, we will be ever badder together. Izzy does not want me to not be safe. We won't run away again because we won't be looking for each other. I promise." whispered Matteo with sincerity evident in those luminous eyes.

The lady stated, "That is a very grown-up thing to know. You surprised me. Who can find your sister better, a group of adults or one little boy? We will have more success if we are not looking for both of you. Your sister will stay nearby for us to make it easier to find her if you are here.

You will be coming here every other week to talk to someone to help you understand what is going on and to understand you better. We will learn and so will you. For now, you will stay with Sue. You owe her and your principal apologies. These you will give later. Now for that promise. How about a pinky promise." And so it was agreed by all. The pinkie promise was sacred and all knew that.

Sue took Matteo to school where he was told that he would stay in the classroom until Sue came in to take him from his teacher. At the end of that day he noticed that one of the teachers or someone from the office stood at the door as students left in addition to the regular teachers who opened car doors and put the students in their cars. New strategies to keep everyone safe were in place. Matteo felt sad that he had made more work for the teachers. Running away was tough business.

CHAPTER **52**

FRIDAY CAME AND THE PENITENT MATTEO WAS THE BEST HE HAD ever been. Sue came to the school to pick him up early. All her other charges were still in class. She said she had a surprise for him. This worried him because he was pretty sure he hadn't deserved it!

They went to that big official-looking building and Matteo was taken to the same room. Sue put him in the big chair across from the lady. She gave him a kiss on his cheek and left the room. Now he was terrified. Maybe they had decided to take him to jail after all. It looked like Sue had left him. Maybe he was going to jail after all. He was trouble, a problem for all these adults.

"Well," the lady said, "we have been lucky to have found a lady who specializes in children who are a bit more challenging. Sue has many children who need her and want to be with her. Your new caregiver has experience with children who are unhappy. Would you like to meet her?"

Matteo thought that all he does now is cry. The door opened and he dropped his face into his hands. Maybe if he didn't look at her this would not happen. He felt and heard someone come and sit in the chair next to him. This person said gently "Matteo, look at me." He couldn't believe it and dropped his hands to turn to this person. Then he was out of his chair and into the arms of Tillie.

"Well, well," said the lady he called boss lady, "It looks like you agree. You will go home with Mrs. Green now. Everything you have at Sue's will be delivered to your new residence. Remember our pinkie promise. Oh yes, we have another surprise for you. You will have another child staying with you and Mrs. Green. Please bring in Izzy."

Tillie hugged both children in an all-encompassing hug. "It is time for pizza." The door opened again and this little group was joined by the other key players in this little drama.

Boss lady smiled as she slipped out. Some days were just better other other days. This day was one of those very special days. She looked back to see Tillie, Izzy, Matteo, Mark, Fjona and Elisha slide out of the room. They were on the way to the pizza parlor. It was time to party!

After a hardy pizza meal, Tillie put her two in the back seat of her top-down red Sebring and headed home.

Dessert was served at home. The children were exhausted. Izzy had turned herself in earlier in the week as advised by Tillie. The necessary paperwork had been done to assign the two children into the care of this highly skilled lady. The school had been notified and both children would be going to school on Monday.

Matteo woke up during the night and felt the furry warmth of Classi and Jazzi. They were there as expected. Matteo got out of bed and checked all around. The tree was so beautiful, Tillie was in her room and Izzy was sound asleep in her room.

He raised his face to his Savior and gave thanks for this little family and added, "Oh yes and there is just one more thing, maybe two. I promise to be as good as I can be. I will never ask for anything again. You are good. I thank you for Izzy and Mattigram." He seemed very relieved and went to his bed. He looked up at those amazing little cars, shook his head and went to bed to dream the dreams of angels.

CHAPTER **53**

THANKSGIVING WAS INDEED A DAY OF THANKSGIVING. THE SPEcial group of Tillie, her wards, Mark, Elisha and Fjona all went to Mark's for Christmas. He introduced his fiancé and asked the two children to be junior bridesmaid and ring bearer for their wedding to be held in the spring. Tillie said it would be fine if Carlos and Maria agreed. Then Mark couldn't help but add that he had already asked them and they had gladly accepted for the children.

Matteo and Izzy were allowed to use the tablet and laptop owned by Mark to look up what these two honorary positions in a wedding involved. They were speechless, which was, in itself, a miracle to be added to the thankful list.

Matteo recovered to ask, "Can Classi and Jazzi be flower and ring celebs, too?" He was bewildered when laughter erupted.

To Matteo, those cats were small children in fur coats. He, of course, had to express this. Again, the laughter puzzled him.

It was agreed that the girls would be invited to the dinner before the wedding. The difference would be that they would have the privilege of a private room and their food would be raw...cat sushi.

CHAPTER 54

SATURDAY CAME AND THEY HAD THE BEST WEEKEND THAT THEY
could remember. They went Christmas shopping and asked Tillie
to let them go into Home Goods on their own. It had been hard to trust
them but then decided it was best to give them a chance. She went to
the Bealls store next door. She had told them where she was going. She
found some cute pajamas for them for Christmas and had them wrapped
before putting them in the store bags.

She heard running steps and saw Matteo and Izzy rushing to her.
They had packages of their own. Twinkling eyes made her realize what
she must say, "Oh, you have bought presents for the girls?"

Matteo crowed, "Oh yes! All our girls! All three!" The joy that em-
anated from them was almost overwhelming.

"Well, Tillie said, "I think we should go for a treat. I talked to your
teachers and you both did perfect work and showed perfect behavior. It
is time for a dessert!"

Such joy followed these three. When they got home the children
insisted that their present for her had to be opened immediately. Tillie
said, "Yours must as well." It is two weeks until Christmas but you will
be able to use them now.

They sat on the floor by the tree and the children opened their
matching pajamas. They were thrilled. They had never had Christmas
pajamas before as gifts were always sensible and within their budget.

They turned their faces to Tillie. "Now you Mattigram!" crooned an excited Matteo.

"Yes, Tilliegram," added Izzy! Amazing, but they didn't fight over the two different names for their Tillie. Tillie opened the present to find a tree topper that was a beautiful angel. "It is ok because it is our allowance for what was and what will be. We saw it and knew it was you. It looks like you and you are our angel."

Then Tillie demonstrated that tears can be happy. She got a chair and with the kiddos holding it to keep it from tipping, she put the silver and gold angel on the top of the tree. She shone with a perfect light over all below.

There was a knock at the door and Tillie said, "Now for the best gift of all. The cats went to the door and opened it. In came Mark, Elisha and Fjona. There was a brief pause, and then Maria and Carlos strode in!

Two days before Christmas and Tillie called the Martinez family to come over for a treat. The lights were soft and the Christmas treats amazing. There was a knock on the door. The door was opened by Tillie. Where were the doormen aka cats? Backlit by the light from the hall the lady standing there looked like an Angel. In each hand she held a box with a handle. Her long hair was soft strawberry blond. Her smile was irresistible.

The boxes started to complain in high pitched calls. Lynda Nelson closed the doors behind her before she opened the kennels. Out tumbled four fluffy balls of protesting mischief.

Lynda said," I have their papers here to register them for you. This classic silver and one white belong to Tillie and I believe that the other two white babies own two children named Matteo and Izzy. Yes, I said own two children because that is what cats do."

Tillie said, "Remember when we talked about having cats one day? I told you that I had found the owner of our two and that she was coming to get them because they had been housed here temporarily. Lynda was picking them up for a show in Tampa. We learned that they are Russian Siberians.

You picked names for pretend cats. Now those names belong to real cats. Meet Tsarina and Casper. Tsarina is the little female with the gold eyes and Casper is the little male with the green eyes. You are now owned by these two fur balls. They are for real!

The white female is also named Jazzi and the classic silver is named also named Classi." They are mine and I will be showing them with my new friend, Lynda. This will be my new hobby.

All that Tsarina and Casper need to make their homes a welcoming place is already set up in your apartment. The kittens are my gifts to the Martinez family." Izzy looked at her mother who nodded with tears in her eyes.

The kennel doors were open and the front door opened again to let in the original Classi and Jazzi who immediately went into the kennels after enthusiastically greeting their owner, Lynda.

Lyda explained, "A friend of mine kept these adventurous girls for me as I was coming to take them to a show in Tampa. I hear they made many friends. They had been here for a show and my friend and I decided that they would stay with her until the next show in Tampa. My friend shows cats for me and grooms them as well. Lynda walked over to the door and put a device on the doorknob to show them the way to keep the cats secure.

Now the American dream was a realization to the children. It was all they had dreamed of and more!

(This epilogue is to introduce you to the breeder of the for real Classi and Jazzi who reside with and own the author of this book. Lynda Nelson is much more than the breeder of Russian Siberians. She is my friend and the owner of Champions. Watch for a book about her and this marvelous hypoallergenic cat. Her cattery, Kravchenko Siberian Cats is located in Port Orange, Florida.)

Printed in the United States
by Baker & Taylor Publisher Services